A House East of Regent Street

Pam Rosenthal

P&M Editorial Services

Copyright

This book is a work of fiction. Names, characters, places, and incidents are the product of the author's imagination or are used fictitiously. Any resemblance to actual events, locales, or persons, living or dead, is coincidental.

About *A House East of Regent Street*

The future looks bright for former sailor Jack Merion. His wartime heroics have won him influential contacts, and his good looks and flair for business are definite assets. With funds to invest, he's on the brink of financial success in the high-stakes world of Regency London.

And buying the house in Soho Square is a can't-miss opportunity. Once a fashionable brothel, the property will yield a good income in commercial rents and a clear path to the respectable life Jack has never known.

There's only one problem – another prospective buyer. With a dark past, a desperate future, and some unmistakable assets of her own, Miss Cléo Myles is a formidable obstacle, one that Jack would be wise to steer clear of.

But instead, he proposes a bargain that's as scandalous as it is irresistible.

Five afternoons. Five rooms. Uncountable pleasures…

…In a neighborhood that's seen better days. And a house that's seen everything except love.

"Pam Rosenthal is a master at her craft and *A House East of Regent Street* is a gem, the kind of gem that is not only beautiful to behold but radiates warmth and unforgettable emotional clarity. She combines the sexiest of moments with the most touching character development and you will be doing yourself a great favor to fall into this story and let it transport you!"

– Sherry Thomas

For my husband, who hectored and cajoled this edition into existence. With love and gratitude.

Table of Contents

Monday

London, 1816

"**P**OMPEIIAN RED.

"Turner's Yellow.

"Zoffany Blue."

The rooms glowed. Rich afternoon September sunlight poured in through tall, graceful windows; the air shimmered as though suffused with the earths, stones, and metals that lent their hues to the walls.

"And the green?" Jack Merion waved his cane at the walls of the front parlor. The room was nearly empty; his voice echoed as he wandered among a few chairs and a settee, discreetly swathed in holland covers.

"What's the green called?" he asked the property agent.

"Sorry, Mr. Merion. I've forgotten what they call the green paint. But it's got verdigris crushed up in it. Lapis lazuli in the blue paint, verdigris in the green." Mr. Wilson's boyish face had caught a slanted ray of sunlight; his cheek was mottled with faint splotches of color from the walls. He shrugged, as though to slough off any personal identification with all that rowdy brilliance.

"One doesn't usually see such expensive paint, but the tenant" – he allowed himself a bit of a snigger here – "evidently considered it worth the investment."

No need to be patronizing, Jack thought. Whatever the tenant's taste or motivation, the investment had paid off handsomely. Situated just off Soho Square, the house had been a popular and highly profitable brothel, maintaining its luster even as the neighborhood grew shabbier and less fashionable, and while more elaborate houses farther west attracted a richer custom. The lease having finally expired, however, the tenant had chosen not to renew.

One could easily imagine this parlor in its heyday: glowing green walls, delicate furniture, bronze brocade at the windows. You'd come here first, to choose a girl for the evening. It must have been… inspiring.

In any case, the woodwork was solid, and the price was likely to be reasonable. Better grab it up quickly, Jack told himself. In a fortnight, he could have a good crew of laborers chopping it up into offices and modest flats, walls painted over in appropriately sober hues. Some proprietors, he supposed, might still try to keep it intact, thinking to revive the house's – even the neighborhood's – past glory. But if you had a sharp eye for property values and social distinction, you'd know there were bigger changes on the horizon.

Because the Prince Regent, like an eager puppy, had lately begun to mark his territory, his architects laying plans for parks and crescents, canals and arcades, and a boulevard to rival the great shopping thoroughfares of Paris. Some of these designs were still merely marks on paper and proposals before commissions, but in some neighborhoods ground had already been broken and populations displaced, to make way for the coming glories of Regent's Park, Regent's Crescent, Regent's Canal.

And most notably, the new commercial thorough-fare. People were already calling it Regent Street. Call it what you liked, Jack thought; what mattered was that the street would constitute a sort of rampart, a bastion of social exclusivity neatly dissociating the city's ton from the remainder of its populace. Lesser sorts of people would still go about their business eastward of Regent Street – in flats, shops, and offices rented from "paper-money men" sharp enough to develop those properties – while the Polite World concentrated its pursuit of pleasure in opulent town houses in Mayfair and St. James. Even the paper-money men, like Jack himself, would endeavor to locate themselves in the West End, establishing families (quite as Jack was hoping to do) in those trim little stuccoed crescents going up in Maryle-bone. This property, splendid as it was, could only be an investment, one that Jack was considering quite seriously, for the rents he could charge.

It was gratifying, he thought, that an ex-sailor could afford to buy such a building. For, contrary to the proverbial way of sailors, Jack had saved what he'd gotten over the years, be it from wages, prize money, or some early smuggling ventures that were now safely buried in his past. And more importantly, he'd invested what he'd saved, choosing those investments carefully, and becoming respected for his judgment. With the result that these days, he could almost always depend upon being treated as a man of means – though he might still encounter the occasional uncertain moment, usually with minor functionaries. It was usually the flunkies, he'd observed – like petty property agents or obsequious butlers – who were most eager to show their contempt for low origins and new money.

Wilson, however, had been most decent, murmuring the obligatory catchphrases like a benediction. *Viscount Crowden's letter of introduction... family well known to our firm... his father the earl in your deepest debt... A grateful nation recognizes its heroes.*

To which Jack had turned his best public smile: modest, dashing, and high-minded all at once. Leaning on his cane in the entrance hall, he'd paused for a moment under the skylight: War Hero, Justly Rewarded, Entering his Sober Middle Years as a Man of Commerce. It helped, as he'd learned these past months, that he so perfectly *looked* the part. The grateful nation found it easier to recognize a handsome hero.

And so he and Wilson had managed a cordial acquaintance, the pale, plump younger man expatiating upon the house's fine design and good construction, while the broad-shouldered, sun-darkened older one contributed an ex-sailor's working knowledge of the inside of a brothel. By now, Jack had quite won the young property agent's affections.

"Someone else is interested in this property," Wilson confided, "to use for its original purposes. A Frenchman. I've been expecting him this afternoon as well. But as he's quite late already, I doubt we need worry about him."

Jack shrugged, not worried at all.

"Well then," the young man continued, "we've seen the kitchen downstairs and the dining room at the back of the house – nice, eh, to imagine the girls taking their meals there? So I think we'll want to go upstairs now." A broad wink. Silly youth, Jack thought.

Having mounted the stairs to the second storey, they found a lovely little bedroom, painted in that rich Zoffany blue. Good, springy Elastic Bed, well covered against dust. Elaborate plasterwork on the ceiling – cherubs, it looked like.

Beautiful house. Had he ever been here? Possibly, quite some years back, during the smuggling days.

Occasionally, after a venture had gone particularly well, he and a few of his mates had treated themselves to places like this, rather than their accustomed cheap haunts in Wapping. They'd clean and smarten themselves up, contain their rowdiness, give the girls a break (as they liked to joke) from the *softer* sort of gentlemen who made up the house's usual custom.

There were additional small bedrooms on this second storey, and other, more interesting spaces as well, like a large room that held various bulky and oddly shaped items, ghostly in their cloth covers.

"They'd do their more public entertaining in a room like this," Jack said. "Pageants and such, they'd be half dressed, singing and playing musical instruments – that's a harp, I suppose, and that thing looks like a barrel organ."

The room would have provided a graceful setting for it.

Though in fact he'd never had a lot of patience for such entertainments; to him the point had always been the fucking.

Whereas for Wilson... The younger man gazed dreamily at the harp until Jack cleared his throat.

"And on the next storey..." he suggested.

"Quite," murmured his guide, leading the way up the stairs. Upon peering into the first room on the house's third storey, however, Wilson's cheeks flushed a sudden dark red. Perhaps a reflection of the paint on the walls again, Jack thought, but not likely.

"Yes, well, and *here* we h-have a… a…"

"Chamber of torments." Abruptly, Jack finished the young man's sentence for him, in a sharp tone that precluded any impression of discomfiture on his own part.

The walls were done in dark Mediterranean red. No windows: the light entered from skylights in the roof. Curious dark panels were mounted high on the walls; wooden gargoyles appeared to be perched atop iron contrivances bolted into the panels' carvings. And hanging down from the bolts? Chains, with wrist cuffs attached. Cranks and pulleys to adjust them, and some odd hinged mechanisms whose workings he didn't quite understand. The gargoyles grinned and grimaced in a mute frenzy of anticipation.

He pulled the holland cover from a large, square object. The tooled ebony cabinet hadn't been shut correctly. Its door swung open, revealing the whips and floggers, the switches, straps, and scourges, neatly ranged in order of size and formidability.

Wilson let out a sort of squeak that might have been a scandalized giggle, while Jack stood silent as the gargoyles, his face circumspect and just mildly ironic, trying to deal with whatever complex of emotion the room had churned up in him.

Not shock or surprise exactly. And certainly not disgust – live and let live; if you paid your money you were entitled to whatever entertainment was available. No, what he was feeling was more complicated, a sort of unwilling envy of anyone so confident of his place in the world that he'd pay for a taste of helplessness and humiliation. Where Jack came from, you got your ration of helplessness and humiliation for free.

The gentlemen who'd used this room had probably pretended to be little boys at Eton again – Lord Crowden had once explained a little of what *that* had been like. Jack had noticed a bundle of slender willow canes in the ebony cabinet. Also a cat o' nine tails: perhaps the gentlemen had also played at being seamen, spread-eagled and stripped to the waist, waiting for the hideous bite of knotted rope at their naked backs. They probably fantasized a whole ship's crew assembled on deck to watch. And very arousing it might be too, Jack supposed, as a fantasy.

Rather less so, as a memory.

"The room is sealed," Wilson announced solemnly. "When the door is closed, no sound can escape."

Jack nodded. Enough of the red room. The two men took a slow, meditative stroll through an elegant bedchamber, all done in bright yellow.

Well, he had to admit that the house had stirred his imagination. And more than that – no point trying to ignore the physical facts of the matter; it wasn't *only* envy and resentment that had taken hold of him. He took a deep breath and exhaled slowly, as he'd learned to do these past few years, in preparation for a battle at sea.

Mercifully, the stirring began to subside. *Some* advantage anyway, to approaching one's fortieth birthday.

"Yes, well, I think I've seen what I needed to see, Mr. Wilson. I think we both have." They could skip the servants' rooms at the very top. He'd quite gotten the idea of the place by now. "Yes, Mr. Wilson, I'll be considering the investment."

Soothing to begin thinking in money terms again. And it was also time to begin discussing his other (actually more exigent) needs in the way of houses and property.

Mr. Wilson? he repeated softly, for the younger man was clearly having his own difficulties in the matter of self-management. Jack cleared his throat.

"Perhaps it's time, Mr. Wilson," he announced, "to move on now. I'd like to hear about some properties more appropriate to the establishment of a household. Properties the young lady I'm presently paying court to might find to her liking."

He laid mild, didactic stress on the word *lady*, his gentle, almost avuncular smile meant to turn the property agent from the dangerous currents of his imaginings and steer him toward the shores of decency, propriety, commerce. The young man gulped, his eyes slowly regaining their focus.

"Of… of course, quite so. I left the list of properties downstairs. And may I congratulate you, sir, in advance…"

"Hah! A bit early for that, Wilson, but you can wish me luck…"

The self-consciously jaunty exchange faded into the clatter of their boots on the stairway. The smooth, beautifully bleached pine boards were uncarpeted at the house's upper levels; bathed in warm rays of sun streaming from a skylight, the wood felt sturdy, springy, and slightly yielding. They descended another floor, walking on good thick carpet now, and gaining the entry hall on the first level.

His knee ached a bit. Always did, walking down stairs.

A mirror hung in the hallway. He straightened his cravat and ran his fingers through his thick hair to order it a bit – or to make it stand up as it was supposed to do. He missed the feel of a sailor's queue at his nape, but Lord Crowden had insisted he get it cut in one of those poetical new styles that suggested a soul buffeted by winds of passion.

His brow was a bit sweaty. The house was stuffy; all the windows were closed. Or perhaps he felt taxed by the pain at his knee.

"Enjoy the knee," Crowden had counseled him. "Exploit it. The ladies love a war wound." He'd been right, in the case of a wound as little disfiguring as this one, anyway – at least when hidden under well-tailored narrow buff pantaloons. Draped in good clothing, his wound was, in truth, rather an adornment. Ladies liked to fuss over an attractive hero; Jack would never have stood a chance with his young lady, were it not for the fortuitous combination of his good looks and bad knee.

Her parents had wanted someone better born. But in the patriotic haze of these postwar days they were willing to indulge her – even, finally, to welcome Jack's daily presence at their house on Cavendish Square.

With his sharp nose for turbulent weather, however, Jack was in a hurry to seal the bargain, before Miss Oakshutt (Evelina, as she'd lately allowed him to call her) conceived a fancy for some other suitor and whatever novelties he might offer.

A loud clacking noise interrupted his thoughts: an unexpected rap at the front door's big brass knocker. Wilson shrugged and hurried to answer it, while Jack nodded absentmindedly – perhaps the phantom Frenchman had materialized after all.

Evelina was a good deal younger than he was, pretty enough, blonde and well-shaped. With her dowry and her merchant father's connections in the City, she was as satisfactory in her way as Andrewes, the tailor Crowden had recommended, was in his.

Not that Jack wouldn't keep his end of the bargain. He'd provide well for her and the children they'd have; act the sober, faithful husband. And of course he'd do his duty in bed – after all, as Nelson had famously expressed it, *England expects that every man will do his duty.*

In any case, he'd had enough of whores and whorehouses. He'd steal a kiss from Miss… from *Evelina*, this very evening.

But what had Wilson been doing all this time?

There were voices at the front door. Jack turned from his reflection, to join Wilson and the new arrivals.

➤➤➤◄◄◄

THEY WERE AN interesting trio: the hugely tall, crag-faced servant wheeling an invalid chair; the distinguished, rather wizened gentleman seated in it – the Frenchman, evidently; and the simply dressed but extremely elegant woman.

Woman, rather than *lady*.

Unless, Jack supposed, one knew how to pronounce the word *lady* with a certain ambiguity – a tone of voice like a wink or smirk exchanged with the other men in the room, to show that one really meant quite the opposite. A courtesan. Or even better, the French phrase Lord Crowden had taught him – trust the French to come up with an expression like *grande horizontale*. He himself had never encountered such a woman at first hand, and so he'd never been quite sure of all the nuances of implication.

But *this*... ah, *lady* could quickly fill the gaps in his education. He need only contemplate her posture and manner of address; it would be like memorizing an entire lexicon – of new uses for ordinary words that her extraordinary presence had suddenly rendered inadequate.

One couldn't, for example, exactly say she was *small*: not with her posture so regal that only the proximity of the lanky servant called attention to her lack of stature. *Slender*? He doubted that the possessor of such a voluptuous bosom could correctly be called slender. She was hardly *young* but it wouldn't do to call her *old* either; the word *ageless* came to mind, but here his common sense rebelled. No woman was ageless – her youth, or lack of it, was always a critical index of her value.

Beautiful? He wasn't quite sure – he'd always thought that beauty brought with it a comforting, disinterested sort of serenity. Well, *striking*, then, she was certainly that. Sparkling eyes slanted catlike above well-drawn cheekbones; her mouth was expressive, the sinuous upper lip curving in a wary half-smile above the full, appetitive lower one. The afternoon sunlight seemed to embrace her as its own, her bright eyes and creamy skin outshining the brilliance even of these surroundings.

And oddly *dignified*, Jack thought, dignified and defiant – though *world-weary* might have been a more accurate word for the bored, rather contemptuous look in her blue cat's eyes, the tilt of her head and ironic curl of her mouth as she waited for him to get hold of himself and cease this clumsy ogling of her.

While Wilson was fairly panting and wagging his tail, like a spaniel begging to be taken into her lap.

"Ah, Mr. Merion, may I present Monsieur Soulard, Prince d'Illiers." He'd put some energy into managing the French pronunciation. "And" – his shining face leaving no doubt as to the source of his energy – "may I also present Miss Myles." She directed a warm smile at Wilson and a minimal nod at Jack, while the gentleman in the invalid chair reached out a cordial hand.

"Soulard is sufficient. The title is a bit worse for wear." He glanced down at his legs, covered in slightly threadbare paisley. "As I suppose I am as well. Do please accept my apologies for our lateness; my health is not what it might be."

The woman's expression softened; Jack felt himself staring at her again, even as the tall servant glared at him. The barometric pressure in the room had risen discernibly. An awkward silence clogged the air.

No doubt, Jack thought, Soulard understood exactly what was going on. One wouldn't have such a creature as Miss Myles under one's protection and *not* be familiar with the effects she'd inevitably produce in male company. But the invalid's manners were as perfect as his lightly accented English, and he cleared the freighted air with graceful chatter. "And anyway, a prince in France is not what a prince in England is. I was, and then wasn't, and now am again, a rather petty nobleman."

The woman smiled and touched his shoulder, and Soulard reached up a thin hand to grasp hers for a moment.

Jack felt a shudder of envy. Or was it confusion? Or only a spasm of helpless, jealous lust?

"And is the house as you remember it, *ma chère?*" Soulard had turned slightly in his chair to address her.

"Yes, yes, quite so. Well, the little we've seen, anyway." She moved forward, to save him the effort of shifting in his seat. "Of course we'll have to inspect the rooms, see how much repair the paint and plaster will need. *And* check against the furniture inventory." She frowned. "They've already sold off some of the most valuable items, you know, like the Elastic Beds: there are only two of those remaining, and a decent house needs considerably more of them, especially for an older custom. But we'll have to see. It might do very well. Mr. Wilson, will you be so kind as to lead us upstairs?"

How casually, Jack thought, she spoke of Elastic Beds. It was disorienting to hear her speaking so briskly, like a shopkeeper.

One expected so elegant a woman to speak in a languid, aristocratic drawl – like Crowden's mother and sisters, when the viscount had brought Jack to tea.

But that was nonsense: Miss Myles's profession didn't draw its adepts from the ranks of countesses. Though he was beginning to wonder if some countesses might not copy their style and bearing from members of Miss Myles's profession.

The servant was evidently going to carry Soulard, invalid chair and all, up the steps. Miss Myles leaned down to smooth the paisley over her companion's lean hips.

And Jack couldn't quite believe the words issuing from his own mouth.

"It *might* have done very well, Miss Myles, Monsieur Soulard. But you see, before your arrival, I was so taken myself with the house's, um, proportions, that I made Mr. Wilson a rather impetuous offer…"

As the 5500 quid he heard himself propose was rather more substantial than any figure hitherto hinted at, a respectful silence ensued. Wilson nodded enthusiastically, not even trying to hide his surprise. Jack dismissed him with a quick glance and turned to the trio, his brows raised in gentlemanly affability, quite as if he didn't already know how they'd be responding to the sum he'd put forth.

Another beat of silence.

"Ah," Monsieur Soulard replied. "Unhappily, it is not possible to counter so formidable an offer."

Unhappily indeed, it being evident that they'd wanted the house a lot more than they'd been letting on. The tall servant bared his teeth. Soulard maintained his elegant reserve, though he slumped a bit in his invalid chair. And Miss Myles squared her slender shoulders and gazed thoughtfully at Jack as regrets and good-days were exchanged, turning to glance at him once more as and she and her companions quitted the house and joined the busy crowds in the street outside.

As IT TURNED out, Jack hadn't stolen (or even begged) a kiss from Miss Oakshutt that evening after all. In fact, he'd sent her a message instead, begging her pardon and professing his disappointment, but he felt a bit peckish and must forgo the delight of her company. A recurring touch of the malaria he'd once contracted in – he'd shrugged and written "Gibraltar." He dined heartily (especially, he thought, for a man suffering a touch of malaria), and took brandy and a cigar in his small, very orderly sitting room.

And waited.

Calmly at first, trying to divert himself with a fat

book he'd bought, in the vague apprehension that a man of substance should have some volumes on the shelves of his home. It was a collected Shakespeare, and Jack, in truth, was rather bogged down in *The Tragedy of Antony and Cleopatra*. Thus far his favorite bit was where the queen, and Antony too, had gone sneaking out of the palace to carouse on the city streets, so silly and infatuated with each other as they were. Any idiot could tell they'd be paying for letting their guard down like that, he thought, though the bloody play was certainly taking its time getting there.

It was growing late.

Had he miscalculated? Underestimated her?

Impossible. There was only one way to interpret her final glance, out there on the front steps.

Finally, he heard a low rap at the front door of his sitting room.

"A Miss Myles to see you, Sir."

"My word, and at this hour." He affected a note of stuffy surprise: *Whatever might the lady be doing, out alone so late?* "Well, show her in, Weston, show her in."

She seemed a bit wan in the lamplight, her eyes dark smudges against her pallor, her body indeterminate in a hooded blue velvet cloak. But still the dignified, upright posture, the dark, jewel-like glints in her eyes. Eyes that might have taken their tones from lapis lazuli and verdigris. Eyes like a northern sea with a squall on the way.

"Miss… Myles, is it?"

A brief nod, as though it were too wearying to evince the scorn his silly charade warranted.

"Good evening, Mr. Merion."

He rose to greet her. "Here, let me help you off with that cloak."

"Thanks, I think I'll keep it on. Unless," she spoke more softly, "you'd prefer I remove it."

"No, just as you choose. Well then," – he gestured vaguely – "do sit down, Miss Myles, and tell me what brings you out so late this evening."

She did, however, let the hood slip back off her hair, which was black, thick, and caught in a simple Grecian knot at the back of her head.

She took a small hard chair straight across from his.

Settling comfortably back in his own wide armchair, he crossed his legs and brought a polite, attentive look to his face.

"You know why I'm here," she told him. He was becoming familiar with that blunt, businesslike tone of voice. "You intended me to come tonight."

He widened his eyes in mock befuddlement, reached for his drink, and took a slow sip, waiting for her to continue.

She let a few beats of silence pass, as though to underscore his boorishness. "You wasted money on a house that you could have gotten for less," she said.

Which brought him up quite sharply, it being a while since anyone had laid into him so directly. "Nonsense," he snapped. "It's an excellent investment, even at the price." Which was true enough, though it did rather concede her point. "But surely" – willing himself to speak more calmly – "your poor petty prince didn't send you here to teach a former sailor how to manage his money."

She raised her chin. "He didn't *send* me. He and I agreed that I had to come; you gave us no other choice. But we'll leave Philippe Soulard out of this discussion, if you please, Mr. Merion."

"Have you been with him for a long time?" Jack asked – mostly, he supposed, to demonstrate that he'd discuss any confounded thing he pleased. Upon having asked the question, though, he found that he was actually quite interested in what she might say in reply.

She sighed, drew herself up to protest once again, and then stopped. And when she did speak, her manner was exaggeratedly patient and condescending. "I've been with him for twelve years. And before that, I spent ten years at the house in question."

Her mouth twisted. "You like numbers, do you? Well, here are a few more for you. He visited me there for six months, before taking me home to live with him. Redeeming me cost him a hundred guineas. He's got a wife in Paris. They have serious differences of opinion –

about France and its political destiny, among other things.

"I was twenty-six when I met him," she added, "a bit long in the tooth even then, for a gentleman to make a fool of himself over. Or so the madam thought."

She paused. "And *that* should give you all the numbers you'll need – to tell you what you want to know about me."

He almost had to laugh – at the catalog of information she'd presented (germane and extraneous both), and the unembarrassed candor with which she'd delivered it. Not to speak of the fact that she'd nonetheless made *him* do the calculations.

He wouldn't have guessed that she was almost as old as he was. But, yes, he could see it now that he knew it. Her lightly powdered cheeks were exquisitely smooth, but they lacked Miss Oakshutt's careless glow. And below the pure line of her jaw, the skin – well, it didn't sag, but you could see where it would, when it finally did. He blinked, suddenly wondering how long she'd been watching him assess her. *Age* – hmmm – *age cannot…*

But what a botch he was making of this. And it didn't help that his thoughts had suddenly got tangled up with the play he'd been reading.

"All right then," a hint of a smile played about the corner of her mouth. "Would you agree that we've established that I am no longer young, that you were a sailor and I was a whore, and that you are rich and I am not?"

He nodded dumbly.

"Good," she told him. "Well, anyway, you're right that I came here to make a bargain. You've got something we want, but luckily... well, turnabout's fair play, you know. So perhaps now you'll tell me what I'll have to do, in return for your granting us a lease on the property you bought today."

But he'd had enough of playing the buffoon in this comedy.

After all, *he* was the one with the money. "Quite right, quite right, Miss Myles.

"But I'm sure you'll be more comfortable if you remove that cloak. It's very warm in here."

Pleasant, anyway, to watch the fledgling smile fade from her lips.

She rose, loosened the ties below her chin, and allowed the dark velvet to slide down to the floor around her. Her gown underneath was pale and gauzy – a very fine pearl-gray muslin, piped in that same velvet, and cut very low in the front.

Oh yes.

She stood in front of him a little longer than she needed to, before sinking into a sort of mock curtsey at his feet, remaining there long enough to afford him a splendid view of her breasts – firm white flesh, delicate blue veins, even a peek at her darkly sculpted nipples.

(But of course it wasn't really a curtsey – he'd been mad to imagine a curtsey, even for a moment. She was merely picking up the cloak she'd dropped.)

And having picked it up, she rose quickly, draped the cloak over a slender forearm, and regained her chair, the velvet flowing over her legs, her back straighter even than before.

Carefully, he reached for his brandy. The glass was cold in his hands, the alcohol hot in his throat.

"Yes, well…" It was time to speak, but his tongue felt swollen. He took another sip, rolled it around his mouth, and cleared his throat.

"You'll meet me at the house at three in the afternoon for the next five days. Beginning tomorrow, that is, of course Tuesday…"

She nodded impatiently, and he slowed his voice, speaking sonorously, emphatically. "Every day up until and including Saturday, a different room each time, I'll specify which. You'll do everything I ask. Don't worry, I've no diseases, nothing of that sort. Though I've been told I can be rather… demanding. Still, nothing you haven't, ah, handled, I'm sure.

"And if you do your best to please me – but I'm sure you will, I'm sure you always *did* – at the end of the week I'll lease the property to Soulard and wish the two of you all due prosperity of it."

She nodded. If he'd insulted her, she was doing a masterful job of hiding it.

(And why, he wondered miserably, had he felt obliged to boast? "Demanding" indeed.)

Not only didn't she seem insulted; she seemed mightily uninterested – except in specifying the terms of their agreement.

"Because of course, Mr. Merion, the rents we could afford to pay you would never make you back the sum you offered Mr. Wilson. But you already know that."

She fumbled in her reticule, handed him a sheet of figures. He cast his eye over it quickly: the calculations were reasonably accurate, even if lacking in a few fine points of accounting. Jack hadn't gotten rich by missing the fine points. Still, she – or Soulard, or both of them together – had grasped the general idea.

"Quite right. I'd be renting to you at a loss."

"A considerable one. And you're not the sort of man who does business at a loss. Let's be clear on this, Mr. Merion."

He narrowed his eyes. "The difference – the loss I'll absorb – is my fee to you for services rendered. I want to be assured that you will do *everything* I wish."

She gave a small, rather Gallic, and very cynical shrug. "If you promise to sign over the lease to us at a rate we can afford," she told him, "you can have me any way you like. As many times as you may *demand*, and of course making use of any of the house's facilities, if you're pleased to do so."

A gargoyle smirked at him, from against a dark red wall, somewhere at the edge of his inner vision.

"Any way you like," she repeated. "Even in those ways that you can't seem to believe a woman could enjoy."

Difficult not to gape at her.

"Sorry if I've shattered a cherished illusion, Mr. Merion," she said. "And oh, one more very important consideration. I'll supply a good, slippery lubricating ointment. Promise me that you'll use it when the proper time arises. Otherwise we don't have a bargain."

"I'll use it," he muttered. There ought to be something he could add at this juncture, but he'd be damned if he knew what it might be.

"So we're agreed," he said. He reached into his pocket and handed her a key, which she put into her reticule. "Three o'clock tomorrow afternoon, in the front parlor, first storey."

She nodded. "Where normally you'd begin your evening, where you'd go to choose a girl. Yes, of course, quite right. We shall begin in that front parlor.

"Don't worry," she added. "You'll get your money's worth." Briskly rising to her feet, she told him that she'd be arriving a bit early each day. To – well, to set the scene before he arrived. If he had no objection, of course. And thank you, she added (though he hadn't asked), the afternoon schedule would be quite convenient: Monsieur Soulard hadn't been able to sustain a good night's sleep lately, and so he almost always took a long nap after luncheon.

And before he could offer his assistance, she'd once again wrapped herself in her blue cloak.

He should accompany her to the door, he thought, reaching for his cane. But before he could stand fully upright, the damn knee buckled. It was all he could do to ease back into his chair, suppressing a groan as he did so.

He needn't bother, she assured him; his servant could see her out.

"Um, one more thing, Miss Myles. Your name – um, I should like to know your first name."

Oddly, given the forthrightness with which she'd conducted herself up until now, she hesitated for a moment. "Will a *nom de guerre* be all right? For some years now, I've been called Cléo." *Clay-OH*.

He blinked. The queen. In the play. What was the line? *Age... age cannot wither her, nor...nor* something...

Cléo.

"It will do very well, Miss Myles – ah, Cléo. Well, tomorrow then.

"The front parlor. At three."

Tuesday: The Front Parlor

*H*E HADN'T SLEPT well.

She'd haunted his dreams, but not in the pleasant, teasing, voluptuous way he'd anticipated. The images flickering against his eyelids had been fragmentary, uneasy.

He was late getting to the house; somehow he'd lost his way. Confused by all the new constructions going up, he'd wandered for what had felt like hours through labyrinthine streets; his knee had slowed him down, perhaps he needed an invalid chair.

Ah, but there she was, just around the corner – well, there was the hem of her velvet cloak anyway. He tried to hurry his steps, keep pace with her. Not too far to go now – Soho Square was just a few yards away. The house's fine front of gray stone and red brick materialized like a ship in the mist.

His cane disappeared, and so did the ache in his knee. He bounded up to the front door, stopping to stroke the thick black curls of the little housemaid scrubbing the shallow marble steps.

Somehow, he knew to be careful; someone had spilled some sort of slippery ointment.

A blue-eyed cat sat perched on an iron railing. It watched as he tossed the housemaid a coin and then it leaped out of sight.

The girl turned a hideous gargoyle face to him, stuck out her tongue, and hissed.

He woke with a pounding heart, a headache (he'd drained the brandy bottle after she'd gone) and a guilty, sweaty awareness of how shabbily he'd behaved the night before. Yes, she was beautiful, fascinating, the most desirable woman he was ever likely to have (in *this* world anyway, and he wasn't counting on the possibility of another). And yes, she could be bought, but not because she'd intended to peddle herself. She'd consented to the deal he'd proposed because she'd had no other choice. He'd exploited her and he'd cheated the Frenchman, who actually seemed quite a decent chap. He'd taken cruel, petty advantage of their evident financial embarrassment. Which is, of course, always the surest method of increasing one's own capital.

But he hadn't done it to make himself richer. He'd done it because he was in such blatant, humiliating need of her.

Which made it all the more unconscionable, an insult both to her and to himself.

Still, he told himself, it wasn't too late to make it right.

He could still invalidate the bargain, free all parties

from obligation. Offer the present owners a fee to ensure that they'd rent to the Frenchman – make it worth their while, even at a financial loss to himself.

But... *you're not the sort of man who does business at a loss*, she'd told him. You're utterly lacking in grace or style – she hadn't said *that*, but surely she'd meant it. You're *nothing*, compared to the refined gentleman I'm used to.

In his mind's eye, he saw Soulard grip her hand, watched her slender fingers straighten the paisley shawl about the invalid's lap. They'd been together for twelve years; casually, unconcernedly, they'd flaunted their intimacy, their mutual sympathy, like a king adjusting his fur-lined greatcoat in sight of a shivering beggar. It was a mortification, he thought, to have barged in upon them with his lonely, jealous lusts. The only thing to do was apologize and make it right; back off and leave them to their poorly conceived business venture.

But he'd never backed off from an opportunity. If he were that sort, he wouldn't have begged a job on a merchant ship when he was twelve. He'd have stayed in Lancashire; he'd probably have died in the colliery.

If he couldn't have the sort of touch he coveted, he'd have whatever sort of touch he *could* buy. And as for his lack of grace and style – she could bloody well think anything she liked of him. A woman who could speak so casually of beds and lubricating ointments oughtn't to be judging him. And in any case, he intended to get his money's worth.

For he'd also awoken this morning with a monstrous hardness between his legs. And – as he swung his body around to get out of bed, dragging the bad leg behind him – he knew that there was no possibility he'd apologize. And not a chance in hell that he'd break the compact he'd bound her to last night.

Three o'clock, was it? He'd probably specified three in order to see her again in the sweet light of afternoon. Or because three was supposed to be a magic number, or simply a nice leisurely time of day to have at her. In any case, it had sounded right when he'd proposed it, but now it sounded a damnably long time away.

Well, how did one usually pass the time?

Breakfast – no, he was still too queasy for breakfast. Wash, dress, have his man shave him.

Walk about town. Aimlessly, and then sometimes with dogged, mechanical rapidity, even when his knee pained him. He barely took note of where he was: Holborn, Bloomsbury... the next time he looked about him he'd wandered deep into the East End, where the buildings crowded so closely upon each other that they blackened the morning sky. The streets were filthy, the buildings hideous rookeries; he kept a firm grip on his purse and held his cane like a weapon. Cold eyes appraised him from doorways. As a boy, he'd learned how to put up a wary, aggressive front. The men watching him could tell that he knew how to fight – one on one, anyway. He hurried away before a gang could gather. Or before his knee could buckle and give him away.

Returned to the City's safer precincts, he lingered at his accustomed coffee house, reading the newspaper and trading bits of gossip about the price of securities and movement of commodities on the 'Change. None of his regular acquaintances were about, but then, it wasn't his regular time: midday usually found him at the Oakshutts'. He buried himself in the newspapers for an hour and a half more, making his way to Cavendish Square around two.

Where he learned (though it shouldn't have come as a surprise) that the young ladies and their mother were on a shopping expedition. The butler didn't try to mask his disapprobation: the oldest miss *had* thought you might be here an hour ago, Mr. Merion, but…

They'd be home about three. Jack murmured something about an engagement of his own at three and resumed his wanderings.

Astonishing, though, just how slowly the time passed when you deliberately set out to waste it. Unless, like Crowden and his intimates, you belonged to one of those West End gentlemen's clubs. Gambling and betting were prodigious time-eaters; according to the viscount, clubmen's conversation was more effective still. Analysis of the cut of a coat or the cuttingness of a remark could occupy the better part of a day. Before you knew it, it was time to hurry out to supper or the opera.

Of course, Jack could never aspire to membership in such a fraternity; the best he could hope for was that someday a son of his... Dutifully, he made his way back to the Oakshutts'. He left his card, along with a promise to call again in the evening, when he hoped the young lady would be free to receive him.

After which errand he discovered that he was late (*just as he'd been in his dream*) and obliged to hurry eastward, across the half-laid pavement of Regent Street, through the raw constructions of what would someday be a graceful boulevard. He ran the last few blocks, limped up the white marble front steps (*no gargoyle scrubbing them, anyway*), put his key to the lock, and made his wild-eyed, dusty, disheveled, apologetic entrance into the green front parlor.

WHERE NO APOLOGY was required. A customer, after all, could arrive any time he wished. He'd hired her to please him, and it was clear that she intended to do exactly that. Yesterday's negotiations were all in the past. Today, she would give him everything she'd promised.

Beginning, just as she'd said, with an appropriate setting. Remarkable what she'd done, just by moving things here and there, adjusting the light, and placing herself at the center of the scene. As though she were an actress in a play, delivering her lines in front of a couple of potted plants the audience would come to take for an entire forest. The house *was* a brothel again, Jack an eager customer, and she… But was it the kohl outlining her eyes, the inviting curve of her painted lips, or the languor of her slouch? Whatever it was, she looked entirely natural: mildly bored, reasonably good-humored, a bit relieved that he wasn't an entirely unsavory piece of work. Because what he wanted – what they'd do in the next hours – well, it *was* all in a day's work, for her.

She'd removed the covers from the room's few pieces of furniture – a settee with slender, delicate legs; a small inlaid table; a lamp. The room was much darker than it had been yesterday; she'd drawn the brocade curtains. Well, she'd have to, wouldn't she, Jack told himself reasonably, it would be indecent to leave the windows uncovered; anyone could look in on them from the street. Still, she hadn't drawn them entirely shut; a few harsh golden diagonals of sunlight cut through the space. The upper panes of the windows were cut like prisms; a rainbow splashed and wavered against the floorboards like the sun on ocean waves. The lamp flickered, the rest of the room seemed huge, indeterminate, a pirate's cave of shifting, unpredictable darks and lights. He corrected himself. Not entirely unpredictable: as always, the light knew how to find *her*. Her black hair shone almost blue; the short yellow peignoir blazed against the settee's bronze brocade, as the words took form Jack's memory.

The barge she sat in, like a burnished throne...

Except that Cleopatra hadn't arrayed herself on that barge with one black-stockinged leg carelessly curled beneath her. Or had a narrow velvet ribbon tied about her neck. Nor had there been a cigarette dangling from her fingers when her boatmen had rowed her down the Nile to greet Mark Antony. If the old Egyptian doxy had staged her big entrance this seductively, Jack thought, she wouldn't have needed smiling attendants, purple sails, or "strange invisible perfume" drifting in the wind.

The acrid fragrance of one black Turkish cigarette would have been quite sufficient.

She took a long draw, exhaled, and smiled lazily at him through the smoke, like a girl who'd had an easy day of it so far and might welcome a little exercise at the hands of a likely customer.

"Hullo luv, care to take a turn?"

Impressive. He nodded, flashing his handsome hero smile in return.

To be rewarded with a quick, appraising glance –

from head to toe, and especially in between.

"All right, then," she said, "a bit of rantum-scantum, then. They told me about you, you see. Said he likes it more than one way, if you get my meaning, sir. Well, why not, I said, so long's his money's good."

Infinitely more beautiful than any girl he'd ever had, she'd nonetheless managed to present herself as a compendium of all of them. He sat next to her on the settee, pinched her breast where it swelled out from the neckline of her peignoir, and pulled open the knot in her sash.

"Your money *is* good, ain't it, darling?" she whispered. "Because the rest of you don't look too bad."

"My money's good," he murmured. "But let's see the rest of *you*, Cléo."

She giggled and moved to her feet, managing as she did so to wriggle out of the peignoir and kick it out of the way. Serene, unabashed, as though they had all the time in the world, she stood with her black-stockinged legs well apart, the inky thatch between them just visible though the fine linen of her shift. Arms akimbo, hands on hips at the edge of her tightly laced corset, she raised her chin, letting the cigarette dangle from her lips. A slender trail of smoke rose from the tip; she gazed back at Jack from under heavy, painted eyelids.

The shift's neckline had a drawstring, tied only in a simple bow. Not that it would have mattered; he could have loosened any sort of knot she might have used to close it – he might actually have preferred a bit of a challenge, to uncover, to reveal, to free the breasts he'd been aching to hold in his hands. Firm, heavy, ripe: he buried his face in them, slid his hands down to her waist and back around to her arse. He kissed and nibbled, sucked and licked and nuzzled; pulled her closer to him now, clasping her between his thighs, his fingers exploring the parts of her he hadn't yet seen, tracing the curve and the cleft of her behind. And yes, he thought triumphantly, she was breathing more quickly now. She gasped, and took the blasted cigarette out of her mouth.

"Turn around," he told her. "I want…"

But she already knew what he wanted to see – the tapering curve, the cleft like one you sometimes find in a perfect white peach, downy, dark, mysterious. In truth, he could have gotten a far better view of her arse if he were willing to let her move a few inches further away from him. But he'd once more taken hold of her breasts, his thumbs and fingers tight around her hardening nipples.

Ah well, it was only the first day. There would be time.

Everything in due time, but first things first. Regretfully, he let go of her. "And now turn around again, to face me."

He moved his hands to her shoulders, in case she

didn't know what he wanted next. But of course she knew. She kissed him lightly, put her cigarette between his lips, and sank to her knees between his legs.

He leaned back, dragging on the cigarette as she undid the buttons of his trousers. Quickly. *Very* quickly, the buttons undoing themselves, it seemed, the fabric folding itself out of the way as though bewitched by her fingers. Ah, she had him in her hands now. Lovely, her touch. And charming, the way she was smiling down at the flesh she held cradled in her palm.

He didn't usually watch while a woman prepared to take him into her mouth. Sometimes he even closed his eyes; he liked the passive feeling of being serviced. The cigarette she'd given him contributed to the effect – often, at times like this, he liked to fancy himself a pasha in a harem, drawing upon the mouthpiece of a hookah.

But today he found himself gazing down between his legs and into her eyes.

She stroked her face against the length of him; murmured endearments – "Oh, but ain't he the pretty fellow?" (Did she really find his cock pretty? Did it matter?) He wasn't fully erect yet (had he disappointed her?) – but he could feel the blood gathering, as his flesh rose and stiffened under her touch. She slapped him gently, stroked him underneath, pinched his scrotum – carefully at first, and then a bit more roughly. He moaned and she smiled, eyes alight with the pleasure of discovering him, of learning his tastes and knowing his secrets. She blew him a flirtatious kiss and ducked her head lower between his legs. Oh very nice indeed – her tongue making long smooth strokes up and down the underside of his cock. He watched the glint of her eyes behind the spectacle of his own rising erection.

What a mischievous tongue she had: on each down-stroke it snaked itself a little further over his balls. Greedy little beast, going at him quite as though she liked – as though she *loved* – the smell of him. She'd taken his scrotum into her mouth now: he felt his blood coursing to his center, hardening his muscles, engorging his cock; he shuddered, his belly and thighs began to tremble.

She caressed his belly with one hand, stroked his cock between the slender fingers of the other, while her tongue – he cried out to feel it – made its slow, shame-less way to the root of his balls, and farther, a bit farther, into the darkness, dangerously close to the cleft of his arse.

A quick retreat from darkness now. A return into the light: he could see her again, licking him slowly and easily on each side of his cock's shaft. More slaps, a little harder this time, now kissing the head that had made its way past the foreskin, and now – oh God yes *now* – taking the length of him into her mouth. Calmly, easily, moving her lips and the soft jelly wetness of the insides of her cheeks against him. Caressing him worshipfully, respectfully – *too* respectfully, he thought. "Tongue," he growled, "more tongue." Yes *that* was better; like a tiny flickering torch in the darkness, catching him here and there – egad, especially at *one* particular place – her lips active and mercurial as well, while he moved more deeply into her, probing toward her throat.

The cigarette, long forgotten, had burned down to his fingertips. He snuffed it out and tossed it away. He caught her hair in his hand; she leaned her head back into his grasp; he wanted to lead now, to control the pace and the rhythm of it, to move that gorgeous, astonishing mouth where *he* wanted it to go… at least before the pulls and the surges and the deep, deep tremors – the inevitability of his orgasm – took hold of him. Too soon. He could feel it coming. Too soon. But then, forever would have been too soon.

Hovering on the brink of climax, he stared down into her eyes, all his senses dissolved into a blue blaze of triumph as he shot his seed into her throat.

THE RAYS OF sunlight coming through the windows were fainter when he found his bearings – well enough, at any rate, so he could situate himself in space and time again. No need to reach for his pocket watch; the sun's angle would suffice.

Her head lay against his thigh, her mouth and cheek close by his spent cock. She might have been sleeping; he didn't want to disturb her. In any case, he liked having her mouth where it was. Perhaps he might recover enough strength to have another go at her. Or perhaps she might simply kiss him there when she woke.

His cock jumped a bit at the thought of the kiss. She laughed, stretched her arms, and raised her head; it seemed she hadn't been asleep after all.

"He's still a lively fellow," she murmured.

"He wants another kiss from you."

A light, girlish kiss, at the tip. And another, more lascivious one, on the shaft, near that spot her tongue was so good at seeking out. It wouldn't be long now; he'd soon be ready for her mouth again.

But…

"Are your knees tired?" he heard himself asking her. "Do you want to give them a bit of a rest?"

"Oh no, not at all. Whatever you want, luv."

But he could tell that her knees *were* tired. Still, a whore didn't rest while she was entertaining a customer. After all, she'd agreed to do everything he wanted, promised to do her best to please him.

And wasn't that the idea of this bargain they'd struck? After all, he'd laid out a lot of money. Her part of the agreement was to guarantee his pleasure. Better, really, if she had to pain herself a bit to give him what he wanted.

And yet...

"Come here." He drew her up to his lap. "*I want a kiss from you as well.*"

She shrugged as though it were all the same to her. But he thought he could see a hint of gratitude in her eyes. He reached to kiss her.

"Wait," she told him. "Unless you want me smudging kohl and lip rouge all over your neck cloth."

He laughed as she unknotted the linen and tossed it onto the floor.

"We could have used those quick fingers aboard ship, to help with the rigging," he told her. "And to help in..." His voice caught suddenly – he hadn't expected her to begin undoing the buttons of his shirt. "To help in other ways," he said, leaning back to allow her to caress his chest – first with her fingers, and then with her mouth.

"I'm not a very good sailor," she murmured. "The rolling of the waves," she planted a tiny kiss below his collar bone. "The bumping," this time nibbling on his neck. "The sudden jolts and movements..."

She stroked his head, tickled his earlobes, nuzzled his cheeks. "All that pitching around, luv, could make me quite giddy," she told him.

"We shall have to see just how much pitching

around you can tolerate." He pressed his lips to hers and then forced them apart with his tongue. He could taste himself in her mouth, feel the hard tips of her breasts grazing his exposed triangle of chest. He bit down lightly on her lower lip – it seemed he'd been dreaming of doing nothing else since he'd first laid eyes on her. She breathed deeply, surrendering the moment to him. If he'd *wanted* to draw a drop of blood, he knew she would have allowed it. But he loosened his teeth, relaxed his mouth into a deep, shuddering kiss.

He slipped his hands under her bum, kneading and squeezing her flesh, lifting her, parting her; she was straddling him now. His mouth moved down to her neck. She shifted her center; he moved a bit as well, positioning himself – for he was ready again – to enter her.

She opened to him; the lips of her cunt were about the head of his cock. He grasped her waist, intending to pull her body smartly downward. But she resisted him. "Touch me," she whispered. "Touch me a little before you fuck me."

He almost slapped her instead. Well, he *was* the one doing the paying, wasn't he? And anyway, he was a man and *he* made those decisions. Well, wasn't he? Didn't he?

It all came from that moment of sympathy he'd felt – for her aching knees. *Stupid, Jack.* Give a woman like her a moment of consideration and there she'd be, ordering him around for her own purposes. He should have bitten her lip until the blood dribbled down her chin.

"Please," she said, "please touch me. Just one finger, for just one minute."

It wasn't much to ask, he supposed. But it was the principle of the thing.

"Please." He wasn't here for *her* benefit.

Still, she was only asking for a minute of his time and his touch. Just his fingers after all. Certainly his cock could spare a minute – no reason to be so precipitous, to fear a loss of control. Not when she was touching the head of it as provocatively as she was, kissing it, so to speak, with the lips of her cunt.

Certainly he was man enough to… just to rub the tip of his finger at the outside of her slit. Lightly. Where the lips came together in front. Where she was swollen, trembling…

"Yes, yes, just like that." She moaned, thrashed about – actually, he found himself rather enjoying the spectacle of her pleasure. Not to speak of knowing just how little it took to arouse her like that. Just a subtle fingertip – had he ever before considered what a mystery the female body was?

"Ah yes, all right. Thanks, darling."

But he didn't like that calm, self-satisfied tone of voice. He liked her better when she was moaning, gasping – not to speak of pleading. He played with her some more – the softer, the more controlled his touch, he discovered, the more profound her response. He ran another finger around the outside of her cunt, lightly pinching the lips, then stroking and petting, as he would a furry little animal. Her face had become pink, her eyes soft.

By now he had slid his cock within her – or perhaps she'd lowered herself onto him. Did it matter which it was? She was soft, warm, and eminently ready, it seemed to him, for some jolting and pitching about. He thrust up into her, quickly, roughly; she cried out, and now so did he, delighted by the bouncing of her bum against his thighs and of her breasts against his chest. "Oh yes, lovely," she called – quite as though he needed *her* opinion of the matter.

He wanted her underneath him now. A quarter turn and he had her lying on her back on the settee; she bent her knees more sharply and he hoisted her legs around his neck. He drove more deeply into her. Excellent – except that the settee was a damn uncomfortable piece of furniture – where was that blasted Elastic Bed she'd talked about? He wanted to raise himself onto his toes, give himself better leverage. His knee ached a bit; there wasn't room to stretch his legs as he wanted.

But even with the knee, he seemed to be managing all right; she bucked under him, twisting and pinching his nipples while he sucked on hers. He could feel her begin to tremble inside. If he could only hold off his own orgasm, he thought. He wanted to see what she looked like at the crest of hers. But he couldn't. He could only fuck her harder and more furiously, too far gone even to notice that one of the settee's delicate legs had cracked, and that the bloody piece of furniture was beginning to teeter unsteadily beneath them as they continued to rock in their embrace him deep inside her and both of them gasping, groaning, even laughing now, in their shared ascent to climax.

The leg must have detached itself entirely: the thought made its slow way toward his conscious mind as the settee pitched onto its back – at the very moment she screamed her release and he discharged into her, collapsing on top of her.

Or to the side of her. Or wherever the ruined settee had deposited them. Jack, for one, was too disoriented to get his bearings for a moment. And both of them were too exhausted even to disentangle their limbs from one another for – well, who knew how long? Except that it seemed that the sun had set; there were no more slants of light coming through the window.

"You *are* all right, aren't you?" he murmured into her neck. "Umm, I must be," she replied. "Well, I haven't broken or sprained anything, anyway. But the settee will be needing some repair."

He shrugged. "I'll cover the cost."

"That's good of you," she told him. "Thanks."

She was speaking in her shopkeeper's voice once more.

"And we're lucky" – she rolled out of his arms and onto the floor – "that we didn't upset the lamp and set ourselves afire."

They stared at each other for a moment, both of them considering that they'd come pretty close to doing just that – even without the lamp.

"But it's already evening" she told him. "I must go. And perhaps you have an engagement as well."

He tried to move and groaned.

"Oh dear, your knee," she exclaimed. "I'd forgotten about your knee."

He laughed. "I rather forgot about it too, for a while. But it seems all right. No, the problem is that I'm weak. I'm hungry."

Now that he thought about it, he hadn't eaten all day. He grinned and stretched. His belly rumbled, and he wondered, just a bit sheepishly, if she could hear it from whatever dark corner of the room she'd disappeared to.

No matter. And anyway, she was likely preoccupied with her own personal adjustments. Washing herself, he expected, somewhere inside. Prostitutes did that. Women's stuff; their business.

Her voice rang out from the shadows. "Didn't eat

enough before you came? Poor Jack, how very foolish of you. Well, what would you think about our meeting in the kitchen tomorrow? I'll feed you up a bit, can't have you expiring of hunger on top of me. Do you care for oysters?"

The rules were supposed to be that *he'd* specify the room. But he loved oysters; the feeding up part sounded quite nice. He grunted. "Yes, yes, oysters, the kitchen." Quite as though he'd had the kitchen in mind all along.

She emerged from her dark corner, carrying her outer clothes and some other items with her. "And then we'll repair to a bedroom, of course."

"Of course." He stared at her, fixing herself up in the lamplight. She'd produced a handkerchief and some sort of stuff in a little bottle, to remove the lingering traces of paint from her face.

And now a loose gown, to slip over her undergarments. She dressed quickly. He expected that she wanted to get home to her Frenchman.

She was looking less whorish – and less approachable – at every moment. Especially after she'd combed the tousles out of her hair. Her face was beginning to fall into the haughty lines he'd seen yesterday. Well, what did he expect? It was only a business transaction, after all.

And as for the cries of pleasure he'd elicited from her – the gasps, the moans, and the way she'd thrown back her head when he'd touched her as she'd asked…

To look at her now, you wouldn't believe that any of it had happened.

Shoes now, and her velvet cloak again. "Well, I'll leave you now, Mr. Merion."

She'd called him *Jack*, he thought, when she'd proposed feeding him oysters. And in fact, he'd rather liked the sound of it, though he didn't recall ever telling her his name.

But *Mr. Merion* was more appropriate to the terms of their bargain.

"All right, then, Cléo. Tomorrow. The kitchen."

THE FRENCHMAN SIGHED and shifted a bit in his sleep.

He was going to wake soon, she thought. Time to turn up the lamp. Georges, the valet, had assured her that the gentleman had been resting comfortably for the duration of her absence.

That's how he'd put it: "your absence, Madame." For Georges could express polite censure in neutral terms and with not much facial expression – though given the rough modeling of his features, a little expression went a long way. Whereupon, having delivered his message, he'd taken her cloak without even a glance at the unaccustomed dishevelment of her hair and gown, or at the bits of kohl she knew were lingering at the corners of her eyes.

No question that he knew where she'd been. Georges knew everything, whether he'd been told it or not.

And – ergo – no question that he also knew quite well that she and Philippe had agreed, calmly and in very few words, on the necessity of today's errand.

They needed to rent the house near Soho Square. It was a pity that *she* had to be part of the bargain, but no more than a pity. They'd each suffered worse indignities over the years: her childhood had been unspeakable, and Philippe had almost died in the Terror. Their time together had been gay and tranquil for the most part, but not without its financial ups and down, its emotional complexities. No matter.

Lovers and companions both, they respected each other. They were adults; when hardships arose, each of them took on his or her portion of the burden.

They kept no secrets from each other. And it was impossible to keep anything from Georges, who gave his opinion unsolicited and free of charge. Which was only fair, she supposed; these days he was virtually working for free as well. They'd dismissed all the other servants, except for a char who came in for the heavy work. They'd waited too long, hoping that a property settlement in France might go differently than it had. And they'd agreed not to draw upon the money they'd put aside for this brothel business.

They couldn't afford anything west of Regent Street; this house was their best hope.

She stroked his cheek. It was pleasantly warm and dry; no clammy sweats today, perhaps he was finally on the mend. His sleeping face looked serene in the light.

Perhaps he'd be able to take some bread and salad when he woke, or even some of the leftover cassoulet. Her mouth watered at the thought of the cassoulet: Jack Merion wasn't the only one who'd worked up an appetite this afternoon. She quite ached, inside and out, from the vigorous pounding he'd given her. A lovely sort of ache, really. "Demanding" was the word he'd used.

Demanding indeed.

Her lips curved into a smile as she remembered how astonished he'd been by her own modest demands. Astonished, but not intractable – well, *that* was a good thing anyway. He'd caressed her quite prettily when she'd insisted upon it. And she'd enjoyed those rough, sailor's hands of his.

Of course, he'd know more about what a woman liked if anyone had ever bothered to teach him. He'd been spoiled, no doubt about it, for being so pleasant to look at. Even now. A girl could forgive him a great deal, just for the sight of that smile. Those wide, light, still somehow innocent hazel eyes too. Not to speak of the fancywork below and his energetic way of using it.

One could take him as he was. Well, *one* could, perhaps. But she wouldn't. She wasn't the naïve, accepting girl she'd once been. She'd bring him round, make a lover of him in the four days remaining to her. She hadn't expected the flashes of kindness and decency under his blustering awkwardness.

No, that wasn't true. He'd turned out to be precisely the man she'd known he'd be.

Four days. Only four days.

But she wouldn't think of it as *only*. These days were a gift, and she'd value them accordingly. Do anything she liked with him – even feed him, if it pleased her to do so.

The prince's eyelids fluttered. After supper perhaps she'd read to him for a bit. They wouldn't discuss the events of the afternoon. What mattered was that she was safe, that his health was no worse, and that they were a day closer to leasing the property. He liked to see her smiling when he woke. She was surprised to realize that she was already smiling.

Forgive me, Philippe, she thought. But I do have a secret.

A burdensome one. It was hard, bearing it by herself. For a moment she found herself wishing that Georges would use his mysterious powers to divine her thoughts.

Her companion opened his eyes and drifted back to consciousness.

She took his hand. They exchanged smiles.

Life was complicated.

Forgive me, old friend.

Wednesday: The Kitchen

RIGHT PROMPT TODAY, he congratulated himself as he stepped up to the front steps. Well, he could hardly *not* be, lurking around the corner as he'd been, anxiously consulting his pocket watch until the hand crept round to three. Pleasant set of streets, actually. The truth was, he found the shabbiness comforting, the buzz of trades and laboring people invigorating. Immigrants made their homes in Soho, French and Irish mostly, the mix of accents and the cadences of speech a kind of music. When a flock of tiny chattering Jewish boys crowded and jostled out of a doorway, he couldn't help but feel a bit of their joy, for being freed from their school for the day. It might be interesting to live in such a neighborhood, he found himself thinking – for a moment only, before dismissing the idea with an impatient shrug.

He shut the door behind him. It fit snugly into its frame. The house really *was* a fine piece of construction, he thought, as he started to the back stairs.

※

DAMN, SHE THOUGHT. He was early. The food was ready, but she could have used a bit of freshening up.

Damn and double damn, she didn't like being taken by surprise.

Still, he didn't have to know that, did he?

※

A SPLENDID AROMA wafted up to greet him: mussels, stewed with butter, cream, leeks, and some ingredient Jack couldn't identify. He could hear her rattling the pots and pans, singing as she worked, her voice thin but sweet. He waited, just outside the doorway, to hear what she was singing.

> A Wife's like a guinea in gold,
>
> Stampt with the name of her spouse;
>
> Now here, now there; is bought or is sold;
>
> And is current in every house.

An insulting ditty, at least to a man who intended to marry. One didn't like to imagine one's future wife being passed around like a gold coin.

No doubt he was especially sensitive to such a possibility, as he'd finally gotten that kiss from Evelina last night. She'd been pleased to see him, concerned about his "touch of malaria," and pleasantly surprised by how well he looked. A bit tired, of course, she'd observed, but that was to be expected; he also seemed calmer, more at his ease; bed rest had clearly done him good. *Well, something had done him good, anyway.* He'd blushed invisibly under his sun-browned skin. Perhaps it was his look of confusion that had done the trick. In any case, that's when he had finally gotten the kiss. Hardly a passionate one: in truth it had hardly been a kiss at all – more like a promissory note, redeemable upon delivery of the marriage contract.

But *now* who was sounding cynical about marriage?

In any event, she'd finished the lyric and was humming to herself while he lingered silently in the stairway, wondering how she'd greet him. Like the adorable slut who'd so obligingly wriggled out of her yellow peignoir? Or the distant, self-possessed woman who'd visited him in his sitting room?

He wondered which of the two he wanted.

Each of them. Both of them. The slut in yellow for – well, for obvious reasons. But he also wanted the *grande horizontale* in her velvet cloak, for reasons that were quite unfathomable to him.

Today, though, she was neither of those women. She wore a different peignoir today – of some pale, indefinable color, what little he could see of it under her voluminous white apron. Her face was flushed, and a bit moist, from the steam rising from an iron pot on the stove. Her brow was furrowed – all her concentration directed, it seemed, toward the mussel stew. She'd taken a bit of the sauce into a wooden spoon and was sipping its contents.

Today she was entirely another woman.

The line from the play drifted, half-remembered, through his memory. *Age cannot* – damn, how did it go? – *nor* something *stale... her... her* – wait, yes, he had it now – *her infinite variety*. Walking slowly toward her, he felt himself smile, for the rightness of the words.

She'd pinned her hair out of the way, but curly tendrils of it had loosened in front of her ears and at her nape. He moved behind her, buried his mouth in the back of her neck, reached his arms around her and underneath the apron to squeeze her breasts.

She made a low, appreciative sound in her throat, relaxed against him, and then tried to free herself from his grasp. He tightened his arms about her.

"I was afraid you'd be late," she said, "and that the sauce would boil away. And I wasn't sure..."

He held her more closely, feeling the warmth of her against the front of his trousers.

"Let it boil away," he whispered.

She wrenched herself free and whirled about to face him. "Are you daft?" she asked. "Do you know what I spent on the cream and butter?"

"I'll cover the loss," he said.

"Don't be stupid," she replied. "You can waste your money however you please, but I won't have you wasting food."

She dipped the spoon into the pot. "Taste it," she demanded. "Does it have too much pepper?"

She could have flavored it with brimstone, he thought, for all he cared. He'd lift her up, lay her down on the table, spread her legs, find out – the only way it really mattered – exactly who she was today.

If she would only stop waving that spoon in front of him. To get the blasted thing out of his face, he tasted the sauce in it.

Blimey. "Did you cook this?"

"Of course I cooked it. I live with a Frenchman, remember. We haven't much money, but we eat well. The pepper?"

"The pepper is fine. The pepper is perfect. The whole thing is perfect. And that other flavor – orange peel, is it?"

Extraordinary. As was the smile she now bestowed upon him, of a quite different sort than any she'd given him thus far. But then, it was a different sort of pleasure she was offering. He watched the curve of her arms as she reached to untie the apron from around her neck. He'd thought he'd only be buying sex from her, but it seemed he'd been wrong – odd, how often she made him feel like an ignorant boy again. You think you understand what a man and woman can share, she seemed to be telling him, but you don't know the half of it.

"I enjoy cooking," she said.

She brought the stewpot to the table. The peignoir seemed to change colors as she moved, shading from gray to blue, lavender to the same fleshy pink as the mussels.

"Well, sit down, then, in this big chair over here," she told him. "We'll use the bowls for the stew, after we've finished the oysters."

Two huge bowls, the oysters still in their shells, a loaf of fresh bread, and a pitcher of ale. There were also quarters of lemon and butter melted over a spirit-lamp. He sank down into the seat she'd motioned him to.

"Here's an oyster knife for you," she said. "And you can toss the shells into the bucket."

It takes some concentration to eat an oyster: to grasp it in one's palm, swiveling the knife to open it, taking care not to slice through his hand instead. And once he had it open, to be sure not to slop the oyster liquor, pooled in the shell beneath the little creature he was about to swallow.

Which saved him from the necessity of making con-versation. *Coward*, he chided himself, but there it was –

he'd bought the right to fuck her every way he could think of, but he was shy about conversing with her across the table while they ate. What could he say, anyway, that she'd find interesting? Nothing, probably. He fell silent, for fear of seeing her eyes glaze and her face fall into delicate, polite lines of boredom.

Well, she wasn't a delicate eater anyway. No more than he was.

And so he simply cut and slurped his oysters, taking time, between twists of his knife, to watch her lips greedily sucking in the gray flesh, the tops of her breasts shimmering above the pale silk of her peignoir, the lines and hollows of her throat moving slightly after she tossed back a shell to get at the liquor and swallowed with gusto.

"It's a very pretty wrapper you're wearing," he told her.

She'd torn a large chunk of bread from the loaf, and was mopping up the brine and butter that had gathered at the bottom of her bowl.

She nodded her thanks, chewing all the while.

"But I've seen quite enough of it," he said. "And not enough of *you.*"

"I'll get breadcrumbs over the front of me," she murmured. "I might even spill some of the butter. I can be a dainty eater when I want to, but it doesn't feel natural. Comes from being hungry as a child, I expect.

Philippe was shocked when he took me on. I'd learned to sip champagne elegantly enough, but as for food – he had to teach me table manners, and I still forget them sometimes."

She put down the bread, wiped her fingers on a napkin, and obligingly removed the peignoir. He tried to control his breathing while she loosened the drawstring of her shift. But he couldn't stop himself from reaching across the table, tugging the muslin cloth down to uncover her breasts.

"Yes," he told her, "much better."

Especially when she leaned over to serve each of them a bowl of mussels.

"I didn't make a lot of it," she told him. "Didn't want us getting full and sodden. The oysters would have been enough, I expect, but that's not really cooking, is it? And the mussels looked so good when I went to the market this morning – I chose the biggest, freshest ones; a person gets what she pays for after all, and I... well, I felt like cooking something today. Philippe doesn't have much of an appetite lately."

She looked a bit shy. He hadn't expected her to be shy about anything. "It's an excellent stove," she added softly. "Very easy to control the heat."

They finished in silence. "It was splendid," he said. "And your table manners seem quite adequate to me. Come here, and let me see more closely."

He licked off a few crumbs from her breasts, like a cat grooming its young. She purred under his tongue.

"Were you often hungry as a child?" he asked. "Or was it just during the hardest times?"

"We had nothing *but* the hardest times," she told him. "But you don't want to hear about *that*."

He supposed not. In any case, it wasn't what he was paying her for. He supposed they could have talked about it while they'd been eating, though. Odd, he rarely talked of his childhood in Lancashire. It was as though his real life had begun when he'd become a sailor.

"We'd better go upstairs, hadn't we?" She leaned down to kiss him lightly on the head. "It's getting late. Let me just fill a pitcher with hot water from the stove. And – ah yes – some of those towels that I left to heat there too."

Silently, he followed her up the dark back stairs to the entryway.

"The Elastic Bed is another flight up," she told him. "I put my gown and cloak in that bedroom as well. I hope the stairs are not a hardship for your knee…"

They'd gotten as far as the next landing when he told her to stop.

>>>><<<<

WHEN SHE'D STARTED up the stairs, she'd found herself

idly trying to calculate how many heavy pitchers of water she must have carried to the upper storeys, her first years in the house. Too many to count, she decided – and anyway, was there anything to be gained from dwelling on the past? Better to concentrate on the present, on questions like whether he was looking at her arse as he climbed the stairs behind her. Or what a ninny she was for hoping that he *was* looking, even if she wasn't at all confident that her body could still justify such sustained scrutiny. Perhaps she would've been better off after all, calculating all those gallons of water. In any event, she wished they could get it over with, climb the stairs at a bound – but that was impossible, with his bad knee and his cane.

Too bad she wasn't still wearing her dressing gown. But, as with so many things, she hadn't had the luxury of choosing. She'd tried to put it on again before they'd left the kitchen. But he'd told her to leave it off.

If she'd been cleverer, though, she might have thought to ask him to precede her on the staircase. which was what, finally, she wished she had done – just as he called out to her.

"Stop, please."

"Is it your…?" She had been going to ask after his knee, when – a bit belatedly – she realized that of course it wasn't his knee that had caused him to make that request.

"Put down the pitcher and the towels," he told her. "There's plenty of room for them on the floor, at the landing. And now kneel down on the third – no, the second step from the top. That's right, you can rest your head and arms on the carpet. But better push the pitcher further away, so there's no danger of upsetting it."

The specificity of his demands rather thrilled her, demonstrating, as it did, that he'd been thinking with some precision about what he wanted. But unfortunately, it also demonstrated that he didn't remember – or worse, had chosen to ignore – the terms of their bargain.

He was kneeling behind her on the step now, his knees on either side of hers. She could feel him fumbling with the buttons of his trousers. Ah yes, there he was – not hard yet, well, not as hard as he'd be, and quite soon too, but hard enough for him to nestle into the cleft of her arse. Nice – she made tiny arcs with her hips, stroking herself against him, feeling him harden between her buttocks – lovely really, to be caressing him like that. A pity to have to stop before he grew harder still – a bit more with each stroke – until he was ready to enter her and she ready to receive him.

But not so lovely that she'd tolerate such utter disrespect of her wishes in the matter.

Lord, but she wanted him. Not like *that*, though. Not forced upon her.

"No," she said. "I already told you. Not without

something to make you slippery."

She held herself still and squeezed her legs together. Of course, if he really insisted upon this, she wouldn't be able to stop him. He outweighed her by a considerable amount. At a certain point, she'd have to give way.

But it wouldn't be what she wanted. And – as she'd be obliged to call off their bargain – ultimately it wouldn't benefit him either.

He laughed. "It's all right. I do have something slippery with me."

"The bloody hell you do," she told him. "You know, you're not the first imbecile to think his spit will do the job."

"No, really." His voice was warm against her ear. But what was he fumbling with now?

He'd curved his body around hers – she liked his weight and warmth against her, the press of his arms atop hers on the landing. He brought one of his hands to her mouth, pressed his fingers to her lips. She'd learned over the years that men liked their fingers sucked – odd how each of them seemed to think he was the only one, too. But she'd be damned if she'd open her mouth, or for that matter any part of herself, under the present circumstances.

It seemed that he wouldn't be dissuaded, as – gently but persistently – he insinuated his fingertip deeper between her lips. A pity, she thought.

She prepared to bite down.

His finger tasted of melted butter.

"Will it do?" His voice was a bit anxious. "I scooped some out in an oyster shell – hid it behind me while you were getting the water."

It would do quite well. "We'll smell of it, though." A giggle escaped her, while he lifted himself off her, to rub himself liberally with the stuff.

"And rub me too, dear, yes, that's right, and inside, as well…"

A few last rays of sunlight slanted down on her through the skylight at the top of the staircase. She stretched like a cat under its warmth, arched her back under his touch. Lightly, gently (how quickly he learned!) he massaged her in the cleft of her bottom, touching, tickling and exploring her, and now (oh dear yes) creeping inside as the ring of muscle loosened to let him in – a smooth, buttery fingertip, and now the same finger, up to the knuckle. He explored her slowly, carefully – still circumspect, and wonderfully respectful of the private place she'd allowed him to enter.

But it wasn't a finger she was feeling now. She breathed deeply, braced her knees against the thickly carpeted stair riser; it was the head of his cock now and it was inside her. Still moving slowly, he sank into her like spreading darkness, each deliberate quarter inch of his progress seeming like a new entry, through a new door, into a new secret chamber – each secret, private, scandalous, wicked and delicious quarter inch of her.

HE STROKED HER, curved his body around hers, hummed and thrummed with the tremors he felt in her limbs and belly. Given the extremity of their situation, he hadn't thought she'd respond – or even notice – when he kissed her nape just below where she'd pinned up her hair.

But evidently he'd been quite wrong about that. Even as she moved in rhythm with the thrusts of his cock, she writhed and shuddered at the lightest touches of his mouth and tongue – even at the warmth of his breath.

He hadn't really believed her when she'd said she'd enjoy it. But he could feel her muscles opening and relaxing under him, and then squeezing him, hot, tight, dark.

He could drive deeply now, as hard as he wanted to, while she gasped and screamed her pleasure, collapsing under him. And now he was gushing into her, collapsing upon her, hugging and squeezing her breasts beneath him, while his cane bumped down the staircase and rolled into the center of the house's entryway.

"I'LL FETCH THE cane." Her voice came softly, nudging his attention back from whatever tropical climes his mind had drifted to.

"Sorry," she added, upon regaining the top of the staircase. "I shouldn't have mistrusted you not when you're clearly a man of your word."

"No matter," he told her. "It was a bit of a prank on my part, I suppose. And in any case you were quite right about one thing: I'm going to stink of this stuff. Well, we both are. Not to speak of my clothes."

"Come along," she told him. "There's soap in the bedroom. And… well, of course, there's also a bed."

✶⟫⟩⟨⟪✶

HE STOOD DOCILELY as she removed his coat, waistcoat, and shirt.

He was bit less docile when she got his boots off. And he was becoming flat-out skittish when it came to his trousers.

While *she*, once so expert at untying and unbuttoning – not to speak of peeling a snugly tailored garment down the legs of its wearer –felt herself growing more graceless, less patient, with every minute.

It was because of how beautiful he looked against the bright blue wall, she thought. And even more beautiful closer up. The sculpting of the muscles in his shoulders and belly, the dark brown hair making such a sinuous line down his chest and downward, below his navel, disappearing beneath the waistline of his drawers: in truth, it took all her concentration not to rip the linen from his hips, leaving the fine white fabric in tatters.

She reached to untie the string that held them up. A strong hand immobilized her wrist.

"Leave it alone."

She stared while he made his own adjustments to the drawstring.

"There you are," he told her. "Loose enough so you can wash me and… and so forth. But I don't take them off."

His wide eyes were fixed on the room's chandelier. Flickering toward the window now, the molding on the ceiling. Looking everywhere but at her.

"I was burned, one place. And then there are also the stitches the army surgeon put into me, after he decided he couldn't get the metal out of my leg."

"You have scars on your back, too – from a flogging, I should imagine. Old ones. Well healed."

"Yes, just once, a long time ago. But I don't care about those. The ones on my leg are much worse.

"I was lucky it was just my thigh – the deck and not the mainmast, if you get my meaning. But it's not pretty to look at. And so I'd rather…"

She dipped one of the towels into pitcher of hot

water. "Of course, if you don't wish it."

Clumsy to have to wash him through the openings in the fabric. She did the best she could and dried him carefully, before taking a new towel and scrubbing herself.

"Do you suppose I'd gawk at it or turn away in disgust?" she asked.

He groped for an answer. "No," he told her finally, "a woman as good at your profession as you are would never…" He frowned. "It's just that… Well, I've enjoyed thinking that you like my looks, you see, even if…"

Even if it was her job to make every man think she liked his looks. She put a finger on his lips, to stop him from saying it. "I like a naked man in bed with me," she said. "And after all, Europe has had a terrible war. Scars – especially gotten as you got yours – are a mark of honor."

"Well, tomorrow, perhaps," he replied.

Tomorrow, she thought, *there will only be three more days of him.* She kissed his cheek and pulled down the coverlet, drawing him into bed beside her.

"BUT WE REALLY must go." Sighing, as she pulled herself away from him, an hour later.

"Tomorrow," she told him, "we can use the bigger

bedroom upstairs. They named it the Royal Suite when they did it up in that fancy bright paint. Kept it for special customers. It's another flight up, but it's got a bigger bed. They used to keep it very elegant. It's a very vivid yellow."

He laughed. "Why not? A bigger bed sounds agreeable."

"Tomorrow then," she said, "in the large yellow bedroom. Third storey."

Thursday: The Yellow Bedroom

*I*T WAS BECOMING habitual, he thought, comfortable as expensive boots or a sideboard stocked with good brandy. Today the prospect of seeing her at three hadn't interfered with his normal round of activities at all. In fact, it seemed to make him more efficient, brisker and more confident of his judgment. This morning he'd negotiated for some shares of a wool merchant's business; he could expect a good return on the investment. His courtship of Evelina was progressing apace: Wilson had shown him a few quite likely properties in Marylebone, and today Mr. Oakshutt had clapped him on the shoulder, quite cordially, in the entryway of the big house off Cavendish Square.

His favorite chophouse was just on the next street. Beef and beer were just what he needed, he thought, to keep up his stamina. Though in truth, it wasn't *only* stamina she appeared to crave from him. Who would have thought that he'd be able to please her some of those other ways? Astonishing to find himself imagining new ways he might touch her, wring cries and sighs and (then, afterward) sleepy, satisfied smiles from her.

Nice to have such a woman in his life – and remarkably easy to get accustomed to. Well, in a few years he'd be able to afford a full-time mistress – not *her*, of course, but someone almost as good. For the next bit, though, he'd have to content himself with getting a wife, making decent, respectful love to her, producing a brood of children to inherit the fortune he was amassing, the solid investments and properties. As always, the rows and columns lined up neatly in his mind: not enough funds to allow him to keep a woman on the side right now, but he'd say one thing for Cléo – she'd certainly given him an idea of the sort of woman to look for when that day came.

Still, why think of that day at all, when today was a perfectly good – even a splendid – day in itself? The ledger pages he'd been imagining dissolved from his inner vision. Why not simply marvel at the changing light bouncing off shop windows as he strode past, the dramatic clouds fleeting by in the sharp brisk air? His blood hummed in anticipation of the afternoon's encounter, his only worry (but mostly he'd kept it at bay) being whether he'd really let her slip off his drawers.

SHE'D AWAKENED EARLY, done her marketing, and brought a load of washing to the laundress. A hen was stewing on top of the range; she'd check on it as soon as she finished totaling the last column of figures she'd drawn up.

Muffled in an eiderdown, Philippe was reading Lord Byron by the fire. Poor darling, she thought, his body didn't retain heat well, and today the air had an edge to it. The year had passed the equinox; it was unmistakably autumn now, even with the uncertain sunlight making a garish show of itself through the back parlor window, illuminating her calculations. The weather was going to change.

But the numbers, in any case, were reassuringly solid. With luck, the new business would succeed. It would be a difficult undertaking, but possible nonetheless.

Of course, she wouldn't be the sort of generous madam a girl preferred to work for. "Stingy old bawd," she imagined some fresh young eighteen-year-old muttering under her breath. But after all, hadn't she muttered similar things herself once? Similar and worse.

Well, too bad for them. Make no mistake about it, she told herself: any girl who worked for her would learn to keep her room nice. And not to expect the house to supply bonbons or other luxuries. She paused, reconsidered. No, a desirable girl would demand a treat once in a while. There would have to be nice things, little presents for birthdays and Christmas anyway. But nothing more; they'd have to depend on their gentlemen for candied violets or Pears Soap.

She changed a few figures, frowned at the higher totals, and shrugged her shoulders. A little worse, but at least the calculations were honest. Better to know now rather than be surprised later.

Still, the general plan was good; all in all, it was a neat piece of budgeting. She'd allowed a reasonable amount for medical care, for example – damned if she'd be one of those madams who were too delicate (or too lazy) to look out for the girls' health. *Her* girls (once she had them) would be able to come to her, consult with her about missed periods, bad discharges, strange itches and irksome rashes. There would be sponges and all the most advanced potions to douche with. And lots of information about how it all worked.

Sympathy, shared information, and a sharp eye for disease were good investments. Just so long as no one expected her to care about the occasional broken heart.

She sighed. Well, it was the way of the world, wasn't it? You took care of others when you could, but you put yourself first.

What was important was her future – and Philippe's, of course. During the hard times one looked out for oneself. And one was selfish and strong-minded about it.

Just look at Jack Merion.

Look at him indeed – without his clothes, if possible.

And in a real bed.

Astonishing, humiliating, and almost wonderful, how much she'd loved having him in a real bed. Staircases and settees were all very well in their way, she supposed, and men seemed to find them proof of a certain impetuosity, but when a woman reached a certain age…

A beam of sunlight shone from behind a cloud, slant-ing across her writing table and blurring her calculations. She pushed the papers away, rather more abruptly than she'd intended. Startled by her sudden gesture, her companion looked up from his reading. She turned to him, pouting so as to create the effect of comic befud-dlement. Or so she hoped.

"Well, it's hard work, all these numbers," she mur-mured. A weak excuse; she'd had very little education, but Philippe knew she could handle a column of figures. Still, she had to blame her emotional volatility on something. Until Philippe's last bout of illness, compu-ting their expenses had been his responsibility.

He nodded. "You're very good, *mignonne*, to take it on. Perhaps tonight I'll be able to go over it."

If she'd made him feel guilty, he wouldn't burden her with the knowledge.

"Of course. Thank you."

The clock on the mantle struck eleven.

The really hard work, she thought, would be getting through the next four hours.

SHE WAS RIGHT. After that it was easy.

For when three o'clock did finally come around, Jack had only to take one look at her, sprawled carelessly upon the big Elastic Bed in a brief bright dressing gown – red Chinese silk this time – her eyes shining, legs spread open…

"Put down the cigarette," he growled. And she had not the slightest difficulty getting him to part with his drawers.

"YOU DISTRACTED ME," he told her afterwards. "You astonished me, the way you looked in that red thing you had on, with your black, black hair, you know, in the middle of this yellow room."

She hadn't closed the curtains. The room was flooded with rosy golden late afternoon light.

Her head rested in the space below his collarbone. She kissed his chest and stroked a finger down toward his belly.

"Thanks, luv," she said. "Glad you liked the red peignoir. It's a bit on the artistic side, I expect."

"But then," her finger was making its slow way downward, "you created quite a distraction yourself, you know, with that big stiff cock you had on you. Right inspiring, it was; I could hardly spare the time to look at your battle scars."

He laughed, clearly pleased by the word "inspiring" but still a bit anxious.

"Though of course," she continued, "you're right that the scars aren't very pretty." She could feel his sharp intake of breath. "But they're really not as bad as you led me to fear."

His sigh of relief was more intense still.

"Truly," she said.

He relaxed against the pillows.

She touched a smooth and rather nasty bright pink patch of skin on his right thigh, where he'd been burned in the pitch of battle. "It doesn't hurt when I touch it, does it?"

He shook his head. "The nerves are dead."

"So I can't comfort you there, much as I'd like to."

She leaned over to kiss the battered flesh, and then to nuzzle his cock, now spent and docile between his legs. "Still, the nerves are quite alive *here*, aren't they?"

"Quite." He shivered.

"But all in all, you're not as shy about showing yourself to me as you thought you might be, I take it?"

"No, I'm not. Thank you. I thought you might faint or scream, you see. Well, perhaps I've been exaggerating how bad it looks, but..."

He stopped, suddenly unsure of what he wanted to say, and drew a long breath.

"Come here," he said, pulling her back into his arms. "Of course, I don't know if I can promise quite so much *inspiration* this time."

She giggled and mussed his hair. "You'll be all right, I reckon. And as for inspiration..." She let the lascivious curl of her lip finish the sentence for her, and he laughed too.

"I want you on top of me this time," he said. "Yes, that's right. So I can watch you when, you know..."

—>>>—<<<—

HE'D COME TO understand that some of the ways she smiled were merely tricks of her trade, a repertoire of pleased and excited facial expressions, each donned in turn for a customer's entertainment and enjoyment. But he'd quickly learned the difference between these and the real ways she had of evidencing her gratification. The way her back would arch, her nipples pucker, her blue eyes turn black and almost opaque, like an opium eater's. Not to speak of how her cunt would open and soften to him, the better to grasp and cradle him when he'd gone deep within her. He'd begun to think that in truth their lovemaking was quite a bit nicer after a day's first go-round, when he was no longer so frenzied, so absorbed in his own arousal.

When he was able to make new discoveries. For it seemed there was an infinity to know about her. Places and ways she loved to be touched, sometimes softly, but sometimes not so softly; there were pinches and bites, he'd found, squeezes and tiny slaps that would delight her. Sometimes, making love to her wasn't a soft business at all.

Making love? Could one say one *made love* to a prostitute?

Well, no matter about the words. Sad, though, that there were only two more days of it to go. Less time ahead of them than the time that had gone before.

Rather like their lives.

But she was staring at him curiously – and no wonder, he chided himself, the way his mind had strayed from the business at hand.

Not that he'd ceased his energetic plowing. But there was no doubt that he'd gotten lost in his thoughts – and it must have been pretty obvious.

He smiled his apologies, putting out his arms to draw her closer to him. Slippery, beaded with sweat, her heavy breasts tumbled over his chest. Her mouth met his in a teasing, biting kiss as he caressed her flanks, her bum and thighs.

She moaned, paused for an instant.

Had she climaxed, he wondered?

No. Not now. Not yet.

For here she was, still tight and warm around him as she levered herself back onto her haunches, smiling down at him in clear and evident delight to have recaptured his attention so totally. Tremulous, giddy with power, she lifted her arms, putting her hands behind her neck to give him a better view of her. For he *had* said he'd wanted to watch her come, hadn't he?

Well then, her smile said, *have a good look.*

And so he did.

If I reach out to touch the tip of her breast, he thought, *she'll explode in my hand.*

And so he didn't. Clenching his fists, thrusting his hips even harder, he stared up at her from the pillows, delighted to share her moment of pleasure, pride, and vanity, and thrilled to help her make the moment last. Spectacular, that fleeting instant when a beautiful woman knew, absolutely and exactly, how beautiful she was.

But now it was clear that she couldn't hold back any longer. Gasping, trembling, she tucked back her shoulders, thrust out her breasts; she was all one sinuous line now, from curve of neck to the hot, tight places inside her. Her face, neck, and breasts flushed bright pink. He heard the low growl in her throat.

Heard her – for he couldn't see her any longer. Now he could only feel the weight of her body collapsed against his, the soft, shivering, almost sobbing laugh in her throat and against his chest.

And all he could see now was the warm dark night, the unearthly constellations of his own soaring climax.

⟫⟪

"I BROUGHT A bottle of claret," he said a bit later. "I could open it if you'd like."

"Ummm." She smiled lazily. "And I brought us some bread and cheese."

They bustled about, producing their treasures and then arranging themselves against the pillows, treats ready at hand. He'd remembered to bring a corkscrew, but hadn't thought how they'd actually drink the wine. For of course there were no glasses in the room.

"Stupid of me," he said, "not to bring some along."

"I could go downstairs to the kitchen," she offered.

"No matter, we'll drink it from the bottle."

"Passing it back and forth" – she smiled here – "like a pair of mudlarks in the gutter."

He took a healthy swig and passed it to her.

As though he'd challenged her, she tried to take as

large a swallow as he had. The wine dribbled down her chin. "Here," he said, and licked it up. Whereupon she licked back – at his cheeks, chin, and neck as well – though he hadn't spilled a drop on himself.

AND AS DIFFICULT as it had been to talk to her in the kitchen yesterday, that's how easy it was today. Perhaps because they weren't staring at each other across a table – he liked sitting next to her, against the pillows; there was something companionable about passing a bottle back and forth.

Whatever it was, he heard himself telling her things he hadn't told anyone, things he hadn't even quite known he needed to tell.

A little about his childhood at first, the village where the men were too stupid not to go down into the colliery. And where lots of them died, too, but he'd be damned if *he* would.

But mostly – perhaps because she'd seen his scars – he discovered that he wanted to explain a thing or two about that much-vaunted heroism of his. Enlighten her, so to speak, about his so-called marks of honor.

"It was never my intention to go to war. When I was young I was in the merchant force, and did some smuggling too – well, that's *really* where I made my money...

"We were pressed into the damn Royal Navy, me and Eddy, a few years ago, one night when we were out carousing in Wapping. I'd rather be on a ship that actually *ships* something – hauling coal, well, at least it keeps people warm, those who can afford it anyway.

"No reason to join up to fight the Frenchies, not of my own free will. To my mind it was bloody all right, them deciding they didn't need a king or lords anymore. I might've been more inclined to risk my neck for England, if the lord that owned the colliery had risked a few guineas, put 'em to shoring up the tunnel down to the mine."

He shrugged. "Not what 'a grateful nation' wants to hear from one of its heroes, I expect."

"But you did risk your neck. You rescued Viscount Crowden, after all."

Which caught him up short. For a minute anyway.

"I rescued more men than him. What else could I do, let them die? Nobody cared, though, that I saved some ordinary seamen, and what did it matter? I couldn't save old Eddy."

But he'd already told her too much. He'd almost told her that he'd thought of Eddy as a sort of dad, his own having died when the mine tunnel collapsed. And, then, given half a chance, he might have rattled on about his dad being half-dead for years before that, the cold silence in the house after Mam and the baby died, and what was eight-year-old Jack supposed to do about *that*, damned if he knew even now… Well, at least he'd managed to salvage a bit of his self-respect by keeping quiet about all that.

She lit a cigarette for each of them, from the lamp at the side of the bed. The white wisps of smoke drifted about the darkening room.

"I expect you're from London," he said finally.

"The rookery in the parish of St. Giles."

Quite the vilest quarter of the city. He turned to stare at her, with increased respect, for her having survived it.

She laughed. "Good of you not to jump out of bed in horror. Or check the sheets for some antiquated lice. I ran away when I was very young. Became a char in this very part of town."

Difficult to imagine her as one of the pale, pinched little girls one saw everywhere, hauling big bundles of washing and pails of water, wielding mops and brooms, scrubbing floors. Or perhaps not so difficult. Something about the lift of her chin, the wariness of her gaze. He leaned forward, to look at her.

She turned her head away. "But in time I found an easier way to support myself, as you see."

"Yes, well, and good for you, too."

"The madam liked to advertise me as a sad case of child molestation – 'ruined by a vile and villainous stepfather,' that sort of twaddle. As though I'd ever even had a stepfather, or any sort of man staying with my mum longer than a night at a time. But the gentlemen loved it. I had to wear pinafores, sing sentimental ditties in the parlor until I was almost twenty, when I finally rebelled against it. I wanted a decent corset, like the rest of the girls. And I hated having to hide my cigarettes."

He'd seen the advertisements the fancy brothels printed up. Crowden had picked up a few that had circulated at his club. "How did they advertise you after that?"

She hesitated for a moment. "As the girl whose mouth could accommodate anybody."

"Not very poetical of them."

"True enough, though. Well, *you're* proof, after all."

Uncomfortable, that. Not that he didn't enjoy the compliment. But he didn't like thinking of all the men who'd preceded him. Especially the one who actually mattered to her.

But he'd agreed to leave Soulard out of this.

He took a long swig from the wine bottle, passing her the little that was left in it.

"It's an excellent claret," she told him.

"I think so too," he said. "Well, we've both come pretty far, I expect, even to be able to tell a claret from a Madeira."

She laughed. "Gin's what they drank, where I came from. And gin's what they still drink. Only thing that makes life bearable."

"And these days you've got a prince waiting for you at home. Done quite well for yourself, all in all."

"As have you."

He'd drunk too much wine. Or perhaps it was the unaccustomed cigarette that was making him dizzy. He told himself to calm down, let her cuddle him a bit between the sheets, allow the mild stirring between his legs to gather some energy. After which time she could revive him completely.

She could accommodate anybody. Advertised as such, in all the finest gentlemen's clubs in London.

And she had a prince in her bed at home.

He didn't know which information he found more irksome.

"How's Monsieur Soulard's health?"

"Thank you, I believe he's a bit better."

"Good, I'm happy to hear it."

And do you love him?

But he hadn't really asked her that. He'd simply, for the briefest of moments, imagined he might.

As though – he felt his jaw tighten – he hadn't heard enough about her and her blasted prince for one day. After all, she was the only one to have a personal connection, outside of the confines of this house.

Rolling onto his side to face her, he waved a hand in the direction of the scars.

"Well, anyway," he heard himself say, "it's a relief to

hear you don't think it looks so bad. Because I'm courting a young lady, and…"

Her eyes glittered above a reassuring smile. "It'll go fine, Mr. Merion. When you marry the young lady, I mean."

"Of course it will," he said as he reached for her.

And if this time she made rather quick work of bringing him off – well, really, what had he expected?

※》》》《《《※

"AND TOMORROW?" SHE asked brightly. Her attention appeared to be concentrated on her image in the mirror, while she cleared the black stuff from the rims of her eyes.

Tomorrow.

Well, tomorrow he should avail himself of the house's amenities, shouldn't he? Do something different, exotic, a little less mundane than sitting around in bed trading stories of their childhoods.

Tomorrow he'd would satisfy his curiosity – since he'd never have an opportunity like this again.

"Tomorrow, why don't you show me what they'd do in that red room? The one with the… the gargoyles, and…"

"I know the room you mean. By all means, Mr. Merion. Whatever you want, luv."

Friday: The Red Punishment Room

"*Y*OU'RE SURE NOW?" she asked him.

"Quite sure."

"And have I explained it all quite clearly?"

"Perfectly clearly. Thank you."

"And if, at any time or for any reason, you wish me to stop, what will you say?"

"I shall say 'rhinoceros.'"

"Be sure to remember it, because if you say 'stop,' I shan't pay it the least bit of attention."

IT SEEMED ABSURD, but she'd assured him that it was always done that way. The more ridiculous the special "escape" word, the more likely the customer was to remember it. And the less likely to say it in the ordinary course of events.

Whatever "ordinary" might prove itself to be.

SHE WASN'T WEARING a peignoir today. Nor even a shift. Just a very tightly laced corset, piped in black velvet.

Black stockings and tall boots of russet leather. Riding boots, he supposed.

Her breasts were bare, nipples dark and erect. Lips painted a red so dark they seemed black under the skylights.

IT'S A BIT like the theater, she'd explained. Not like real life at all. A girl who's good at it takes you to a place that's safe and dangerous at the same time.

Are you good at it? he'd asked.

What do you think? she'd asked in return.

"WELL THEN," SHE said. "Take off those clothes, boy. And be quick about it."

He stared at her, surprised. Somehow he'd expected her to undress him.

"Boy?" Her voice was like ice.

"Oh, yes, sorry." He unknotted his cravat.

"Yes, *Miss Myles.*"

"All right, yes, Miss Myles. I'm sorry."

"You're sorry, *Miss Myles.*"

"I'm sorry, Miss Myles."

"*How* sorry, boy?"

"I'm *very* sorry, Miss Myles. Please forgive me, Miss Myles."

She nodded, barely countenancing his apology, and far more interested, it seemed, in how expeditiously he'd be able to peel his clothes off.

Which wouldn't be easy with his hands so sweaty. Amazing what a fuss he'd made yesterday, about revealing his scars to her. "You can sit on the floor," she told him, "to remove your boots."

This time he formulated his thanks so as not to require correction. He was quite sincere, too; if she hadn't allowed him to sit on the floor, his knee wouldn't have allowed him to maintain his balance.

How stately she looked; she seemed to tower over him while he grubbed about on the floor. It would be easy, he thought, to forget how small she really was.

But one wouldn't want to keep her waiting. Finally disencumbered of the boots, he scrambled to his feet to tear off his trousers, drawers, and stockings. And now to stand quite naked – he felt graceless, and ridiculously, gratuitously tall – endeavoring to maintain an air of calm as he awaited her pleasure.

He could hide the feelings of vulnerability. What he couldn't hide was how arousing he found it all.

Her lip curled. "Well, at least *part* of you knows how

to show some respect for what we're about."

"Beg pardon, Miss Myles, but what *are* we about?"

"We're going to auction you off, boy. This is an Arabian bazaar, and you're about to be sold into servitude."

She reached a slender finger to touch him, where the base of his cock met his scrotum. Only a finger, and a bit carelessly, as one might diddle a cat at the bottom of its ear.

He felt himself growing harder.

She laughed softly and pinched him. Not so softly now. "Wise of you not to inquire what sort of servitude. Or perhaps you've already guessed."

The room had a different look to it than when he'd first encountered it – had it only been three days ago? The light from the glass panes in the roof was livid, almost green; there was a storm imminent outside. She'd made a nice, crackling fire in the grate; he could see flames reflected in the polished surface of her boots. She held a black riding crop in her hand.

Pacing in front of the fire, she weighed the slender black rod in her palm. Frowning now, testing its balance: something about it didn't satisfy her.

She stopped her pacing to open the ebony cabinet. She looked to be considering alternatives to the riding crop. Her concentration was intense; to all appearances it was as though she'd quite lost interest in *him*.

He studied the apparatus on the wall opposite to where he stood. A pair of chains – wrists cuffs attached to the ends – dangled down to… well, to approximately the level of his wrists, in point of fact. Three days ago he hadn't fully grasped the mechanics of the contraption, but in fact it was quite simple. She'd be able to adjust the length of the chains with a pulley, loop it over a hook, and lock it – lock *him* – smartly into place.

A certain hinged mechanism had particularly confused him when he'd first looked at it. But the design was clear enough now: the chains could be adjusted to hang at various distances out from the wall. Some customers might be immobilized with their bums or bellies pressed up against the stained red surface; he, however, would not. He wouldn't have that protection; she'd be able to get at him from all sides.

"Ah yes, much better." She closed the cabinet, grinned, and held up a slender branch of rattan. She swung it once or twice so that he could hear it whistle. He felt a bit dizzy: the fire was too hot. Or the scent of myrrh – perhaps it lay too heavy on the air.

➤➤➤❋◀◀◀

IT'S NOT REALLY a matter of pain, she'd told him. Although for a certain type of gentlemen the pain makes it real; sometimes one has to swat at them until one's arm is ruddy exhausted.

But a man like you, who's been flogged in the way of naval discipline... No, I don't think so.

What you want is a certain quality of attention. Well, you'll understand soon enough. Just don't think I won't take a swipe at you now and again.

⟫⟫✳⟪⟪

FEIGNING MORE CALM than he felt, he stared into her black-rimmed eyes. He wouldn't look frightened or ask for mercy.

She stared back at him. "Turn around."

"Just to make things clear." She whispered it in his ear, as though someone might overhear. She took a step backward then, and gave him smart taste of the rattan, right across his bottom.

Clear enough.

"Turn around again, to thank me," she said; he complied quite correctly – even rather elegantly, he thought.

"Now keep your eyes down. Head up though, and back straight... Yes, that's right... That's very pretty. We like a modest boy here, one who keeps his eyes lowered.

"There will be no looking at my face, do you understand?"

"Yes, Miss Myles. I understand, Miss Myles." Obediently, he directed his gaze at her boots, her slender thighs, skin very white above the lace tops of her black stockings.

Hard not to be permitted to look at her face, but in truth he was grateful for the limitations she'd imposed upon his gaze.

Better to focus on her commands, concentrate on her low, icy, precisely pitched voice.

⟫⟩⟩⟨⟨⟪

IT'S THE VOICE, *she'd told him earlier. You'd be surprised how much of it depends upon the voice.*

He hadn't believed it at the time.

⟫⟩⟩⟨⟨⟪

"OVER THERE NOW." She pointed the switch toward a spot on the floor, near the shadow cast by the dangling chains.

"Open your mouth," she told him after he'd situated himself correctly.

"Here." She placed the rattan between his lips, crosswise – he must look like a dog, he thought, with a bone. "Hold this for me, boy, until I need it again. And mind you don't get it all nasty with drooling. Nor put any tooth marks on it."

Fascinating – astonishing, in fact, how important it seemed to be, to follow her instructions. To hold the switch tightly between his lips and keep it perfectly dry.

No teeth marks – well, he'd always wondered how a woman… All a matter of concentration, he expected.

He concentrated mightily on the task, while she grasped his right wrist and proceeded to shackle him.

His left wrist now. She was amazingly deft with the buckles and obviously familiar with the machinery; his arms were hoisted overhead and his body secured into place before he quite realized it had happened. He was glad to discover that the restraints helped him steady himself; he'd worried about being on his feet for so long without his cane.

She took the switch from beneath his lips and inspected it. No spit or teeth marks on it, none that *he* could see, anyway. He found himself hoping for a word of commendation, but none seemed to be forthcoming.

"What's your name, boy? The ladies want to know."

"Jack, Miss Myles, my name's Jack. And the ladies? Beg pardon, Miss Myles, but who are the ladies?"

"Curious, are you, Jack?" She lifted his cock with the tip of the reed.

He wouldn't gasp or moan, he told himself. Not yet, anyway.

Not until she forced it out of him.

"Good boy, showing a little control."

More difficult, though, if she were to continue to diddle him in that humiliating way. He'd rather have another swat across the bottom.

He got one.

And decided he might prefer to be diddled.

"The ladies," she said, "well, they're fantasy ladies, in a fantasy harem, bored with waiting for the fantasy sultan's attention. The sultan doesn't officially ratify this practice, of course; you won't find it in any of the literature. But from time to time he looks the other way and allows them a diversion. And so they need a likely boy, a ready, *demanding* sort of boy…"

She chuckled.

"They're insatiable, Jack. The one who gets you will keep you busy from morning till night. And they're rich, they don't have any real money, of course – well, why would you need money in a harem? But there are the jewels, you see. They'll pay me a thief's ransom in jewels, for the right boy. A pretty, well-trained boy…"

TO BRING IT off correctly, she'd explained, a girl would have to know a bit about the customer. Sometimes they might have a drink or two together, so she can ask him a few questions, find out what's important to him. She looks for ways he's a bit weak, you see, fearful, or vain. Just enough so she'll know what to say.

Make it feel real to him – personal, you know – for all that it's just pretend.

It's not that difficult, she'd added. Not so much as you might think, anyway.

"WE CAN SEE how pretty you are, Jack. It's a scandal, such thick eyelashes on a man – yes, they're quite lovely, especially when you keep your eyes down so sweetly and modestly. And that smile – that shy, honest English yeoman smile of yours, practiced it hard enough over the years, I reckon – got you out of more than one scrape and lately it's made you rather a pet of the ton, hasn't it?

"Smile for the ladies, Jack."

Absurd to be flashing his teeth at an imaginary audience. But it wasn't difficult. It didn't even feel strange to be doing it. It felt to him that he'd been smiling his modest, boyish smile all over London, ever since Lord Crowden had taken him up.

"Now turn, bend. Straighten up now, stand sideways so they can see how nice and tall we've got you at attention."

Still cold and controlled, she raised her voice a bit, as though projecting it outward, to a crowd.

"With a smile and a cock like that, ladies, who could resist him?"

She'd created a perfect illusion. He could almost see

the harem ladies' large, liquid, darkly painted eyes peering from beneath sequined veils, the bangles sparkling at their wrists; almost hear their appreciative murmurs, catch a few whispers and giggles.

And perhaps a few hisses as well, from the gargoyles.

She made a slow circle around him, stopping to display him from different angles, prod him into position with maddening little touches of the switch.

"Lovely shoulders, he's a strong one. And" – shoving his legs open with the toe of her boot – "may I invite you ladies to turn your attention to the well-developed musculature of the arse and thighs? He can move it, I'll tell you, and then move it some more – it's like a fine piece of engineering, a modern improved steam pump, fully operational and not just for show. Wiggle your arse for the ladies, Jack; grind your hips: show 'em how you'll pump 'em."

He couldn't. He wouldn't.

"What, suddenly shy? Or simply in need of a bit of instruction?"

At which point she used the switch to prove to him that he could – and *would* – wiggle, grind, and pump as hard and as long as she wanted him to.

And that he would thank her for every stroke of punishment – or *instruction*, as she'd begun to call it. He would thank her loudly, clearly, and not forgetting to address her with respect and of course as Miss Myles.

He would. And did.

His face and neck were hot. Partly from the pain, though in fact her hand was very controlled; he was sure she hadn't broken the skin. But mostly it was the embarrassment: the exposure – almost, he thought, like there really was an audience watching. A human audience, and not just the gargoyles, grinning and grimacing at him from their perch on the molding.

And not just her, strutting in front of him so cruelly and deliciously.

It's like a play, he reminded himself. *It's not real.*

Damn if it didn't feel real, though. Real enough to make him sweat. And keep him achingly erect as well. She gave a low laugh. Her voice was soft. He had to strain to hear it now.

"Well, we can all see how pretty he is, and strong too, but pretty comes cheap, and strong isn't hard to find either. And I won't lie to you ladies – he's not as young as some boys you could buy for a similar price.

"He's had some experience, life has got to him, for all that he's still a boy some ways, and sometimes" – a light swat of the rattan here – "in need of correction. But a taste of life mellows a person, don't you agree, a little life experience could be a good thing, depending on your taste…

"Still, we come to the important thing now, the thing that will make our Jack a prize for some rich, lucky lady. Some very fortunate lady, oh yes, the lady who…

"Well, the fact of the matter is that our Jack is the rare sort of man who enjoys providing a lady with some pleasure for herself.

"Of course, he didn't know it himself until quite recently, but he takes instruction well, you see, as I shall demonstrate…"

⟫⟫⟫⟪⟪⟪

HER VOICE SEEMED to falter here.

But perhaps, he thought, it was only a different sort of theatrics. A trap set for him, to make him raise his eyelids after he'd been forbidden it. He waited.

"I… I've trained him myself, and he… well, it'll be a pleasure to hand him over to someone who…"

Her voice was fading.

He stared at her. She looked very small, her painted face pale and almost childlike, framed by tousled black curls.

Frightened.

"Rhinoceros," he said.

She gaped at him as though stunned.

Stupid word. Ridiculous word. *"Rhinoceros!"*

For good measure he yelled, "Stop!"

And then, "Damn it, Cléo, get me out of this rig!

"Come on, that's a good girl, yes, that's right, now

unhook the other one…"

He had his arms around her. She was shivering. "What is it?" he said. "Are you ill?"

"P-perhaps," she whispered. "I don't know. My corset's awfully tight, perhaps…"

"I'm putting you to bed," he told her.

Easiest simply to pick her up, carry her into the yellow room, and deposit her on the bed. Later, of course, he'd marvel that he'd managed all that without his cane to lean on, but right then, the only thing in his mind was to get her off her feet – to pull off her boots, loosen her corset. Hell, take it off entirely; luckily, the strings were tied in a bow that was easy to undo. Take off her stockings too, and tuck her under the covers. She'd told him, before they started, that there was a flask of water in the red room. He fetched it now, held it to her lips.

Her eyes were dark, defeated. He kissed the ashy skin beneath them, the soft flesh below her chin.

He got into bed with her, pulled the coverlet over them both.

Hugging her to him, he tried to restore some warmth and vivacity to her trembling body.

Her voice came in a hoarse whisper. "I am *so* sorry. I don't know what happened to me. What must you think?"

"I don't think anything. You laced yourself too tightly, that's all. Tried too hard to give me an adventure.

Exhausted yourself, I expect. For a while, though, it was astonishing. You were astonishing."

"I lost control. For a moment I thought I was going to faint. What would have happened to us, Mr. Merion, if I'd fainted while you were chained up like that?"

"I would have had to wait until you revived. Awkward, standing about like that, but hardly life-threatening. And then I would have yelled out the escape word, just as you told me to do, and you would have freed me, just as you did. Don't worry. We're both all right."

She started to say something. He held her tighter.

"And don't call me Mr. Merion. Jack's my name. Call me Jack."

"You're being very good. But I failed. I didn't keep my end of our bargain."

"It wasn't a just bargain I imposed upon you."

SHE DIDN'T SAY anything in response.

It was up to him, he expected, to free her from the obligation, propose a rent Soulard could afford, sign the papers and wish them... What had he said, last Monday night? Ah yes, he'd pompously and sanctimoniously told her he'd *wish them all due prosperity of the property*.

And never see her again.

"It was unjust," he repeated, "unkind, and certainly ungentlemanly, but then, I never pretended to be a gentleman, did I?

"And so I shall hold you to the agreement. You've pleased me very well these past four days. Don't protest – yes, even today, for all its strangeness. Today was…"

The sound of falling rain saved him from having to find a word to describe what had gone on today.

"Has the rain just started up?" he asked.

"No, it's been falling for some time."

"I hadn't noticed."

"It began very lightly," she told him. "But I believe it will be quite…" She laughed. "Silly of me, to tell a sailor when to expect a storm. As silly as leaving the window open."

Wonderful to hear her laugh.

Wonderful simply to be in the same bed, under the same coverlet, the same good, strong roof.

"I'm glad you left it open," he said. "I like how the city smells when the weather's stormy."

They lay quietly, listening to salvos of rain beating down across roofs and eaves. Together, they breathed the smells of wet paving stones and of drenched leaves blown from their branches.

They held each other beneath the covers.

He could feel the marks in her flesh, impressions the

too-tight corset had left on her flanks and lower back. He'd noticed them earlier, when he'd unlaced her. He lifted the coverlet, to look at her. To kiss the angry red ridges. To use his lips and fingers and all his senses to try to understand who she was – in the small ways available to him, by deciphering the marks her life had left upon her.

"I like a naked woman in my bed." His whisper was barely audible above the rain, the winds and the shuddering of the trees.

They made slow silent love, in the warm yellow room.

⇒⟫⟪⟪⟨

THE WINDS HAD calmed somewhat but the rain was still falling when they finally wrested themselves apart.

She dressed herself quickly.

"Don't go," he pleaded. "Stay the night. You'll catch your death in all that wet."

Lord Crowden had invited him to a late supper. Well, damn Lord Crowden then.

"I can't stay," she told him. "Philippe would be anxious. And as for getting home, there's a cab waiting downstairs. At least I hope there is. The driver knows to wait for me, should I be a bit detained."

"A cab. Yes, of course. I haven't been thinking how

you get yourself home these dark early evenings. Well, you've run up quite a few additional expenses in the course of this week, haven't you? We can settle them up…"

She smiled. "You keep excellent accounts, Jack."

He supposed he did.

It was only after she'd gone, and as he was dressing for his supper with Lord Crowden, that he realized they hadn't decided upon a room in which to meet tomorrow.

CROWDEN WAS IN one of his peevish tempers tonight. Perhaps due to the effect of the filthy weather on a new pair of breeches. Or because he'd spent the greater part of the afternoon being hauled over the coals by his father's man of business – such a bore, he grumbled, and for absolutely the most trifling set of debts. As if a gentleman of spirit needed to concern himself with such matters.

"Though," he said now, nodding to the servant to refill his and Jack's glasses, "it appears that *you* have taken quite brilliantly to such matters." His eyes narrowed. "Or so our solicitor informs me. Wonderful, Jack, the head you have for money."

News traveled quickly through London's commercial circles. The building, the shares in the wool business: the week's investments had evidently met with the family solicitor's approval.

Jack nodded dutifully, painfully aware that Crowden wasn't finding him nearly so much fun to take around as when he'd been charmingly ignorant of which fork or glass to pick up. And when he'd come to supper well supplied with a sailor's ribald anecdotes, more humorous and adventurous in the telling than it had been in the living.

Tonight, in fact, as his lordship was making increasingly clear, Jack was no fun at all, having so little to say about buying the building that had been a brothel, and offering only a weak smile when Crowden, in high hilarity, proposed that Jack go into the brothel business himself.

"If I weren't temporarily financially embarrassed, we could do it together, take the profits out in trade, what?" He took a pinch of snuff and proffered the chased silver box.

"Thank you, my lord, no snuff."

Permissible to refuse the snuff. But Crowden's condescending jibes were not to be challenged. Best to continue wooden, polite, and noncommittal, while the viscount prattled on, enthralled by his fancy of "taking it out in trade" – which was, after all a fancy that Jack had to admit he'd also entertained, before dismissing it as an insult – to himself, and to… well, to everything that had gone on this past week.

Too bad he couldn't tell his lordship any of *that*. Accompanied by a swift kick to the seat of those new breeches.

But he couldn't. And anyway, there was no need. For the truth was simpler, if rather bleaker.

He didn't want her that way.

Five days and five days only were all that he'd contracted for. And tomorrow, the last day left to him, was all he wanted. Before embarking on the steady, responsible, prosperous life course he'd so proudly, so carefully and joylessly charted for himself.

Saturday, and the Days Following...

$\mathcal{B}$UT WHERE WAS she? He'd arrived early today, but by now – he checked his watch – yes, it was past three. Only a minute and a half past, but unquestionably past the hour. He owned a very good watch and he kept it precisely set. The fact was that she was late.

He paced the entrance hall.

At ten past, he began to grow angry.

When bells chimed half three, he became alarmed.

Five minutes later he forced himself to think clearly.

He'd go to the property office, find Wilson if need be, see if they had an address for Soulard. He assured himself that it was very likely – yes, of course there would be an address, or at least some general sense of where they lived.

Find her. Perhaps she was in trouble. Perhaps the Frenchman's health...

For the first time, he considered that Soulard might not be well at all. And that she'd spent the past afternoons here in this house, rather than at home with her companion. According to their bargain, she'd had to. She hadn't had any choice in the matter.

Selfish. Even cruel, he thought. And he'd do it again if he could.

Cane in hand and hat on his head, he was on his way to the door when he heard it rattling from the outside.

He felt vast relief. Followed by fury. How dared she cause him such anxiety? A rap, now, on the brass knocker – had she lost her key? He opened the door.

The tall French valet informed him that Monsieur Soulard, Prince d'Illiers, had died in his sleep. Sometime around dawn, they thought.

Madame hadn't sent any other message. No, none at all.

THE PROPERTY OFFICE did have an address. He sent a letter of sympathy. Well, what else could he do? Anyway, she knew where to find him.

And indeed, he arrived at the house at precisely three the next day. He didn't expect to see her, but his own attendance nonetheless made him feel as though he was keeping faith. They had an agreement. Was he deceiving himself, or did they have something more than an agreement?

He wandered up and down stairs and through the empty rooms. The kitchen was scrubbed, the pots all hanging from their hooks; the only reminder of their feast was a coil of orange rind on the deal table, shedding a faint sweetness as it dried.

I was a char, in this very neighborhood.

In the front parlor, the poor little settee lay supine under its holland cover. He was glad they'd broken it; if he could do it again, he'd break a few more pieces of furniture, create further havoc as a record of what had gone on here.

Touch me. Touch me a little before you fuck me.

He paced the room, breathing the stale residue of cigarette smoke.

⟫⟫⟫⟪⟪⟪

THE NEXT DAY he arrived at noon. And earlier still, the following day. In case she came looking for him. He wanted… well, he really didn't know *what* he wanted.

He stopped reading the newspapers. Notes, invitations, and inquiries piled up unread in the front hall of his lodgings. His life had narrowed to this single daily errand. To come here. To wait.

⟫⟫⟫⟪⟪⟪

IT HADN'T BEEN so bad, she thought, while she'd been occupied with the funeral – the arrangements, and then the thing itself; it was gratifying how many of their friends, and even some neighbors, came to pay their respects. They'd had a small, affectionate circle, mostly French. Some, émigré nobles like Philippe, had chosen to remain in England even after the war ended and the monarchy was restored. Others were from Huguenot families – their great-grandparents had immigrated, establishing homes and businesses in Soho more than a century before. Some of the women had started out like her – don't worry, her friend Christine had told her, you won't go unprotected, we'll make up a list of likely gentlemen, we'll drink coffee and we'll talk. Next week, *chérie*, when you're up to it.

She wasn't worried.

She was stunned rather, aghast and even a bit amused by the spectacle of her own foolishness. *All that plotting and planning, the columns of figures, the care she'd taken to prepare for every eventuality – except this one, the most likely one, the one that had been staring her in the face all the time.* She hadn't seen it coming. Her mind had simply refused to countenance the possibility. And then, those few last days – well, during those days with Jack Merion, she hadn't considered anything except her secret, and her guilty and probably futile attempts to hide it.

Had Philippe known he was dying?

Had he guessed the other thing as well?

All too likely, on both counts. He'd been a clever and

an honest man. And he'd been so in love with her that he'd contented himself with her friendship, her admiration, and the pleasure she took in his company, both in and out of bed.

Nothing sharpens the senses like inequity in love. It's a hard thing, she thought, when the person less loved possesses the finer sensibility. Philippe had undoubtedly known what she'd been feeling these past few days. Probably he'd been able to smell the happiness still clinging to her body, even when she'd bathed herself – scrubbed herself raw – after returning from Soho Square.

How alone he must have felt, in his silent, tactful intimations.

How selfish she'd been, in her stupid, guilty happiness. And given the chance, she'd do it again.

She'd explain the whole thing to Christine and Bernadette, tomorrow, over very strong coffee. Her woman friends would understand, she thought.

⊱✦⊰

TOMORROW, JACK TOLD himself, he'd give up this hopeless vigil. Tomorrow he'd pay Evelina a visit, see if he could explain away the week's inattention. He supposed another attack of malaria would serve well enough.

Tomorrow he'd also see about subdividing the

house and putting it up for rent. Tomorrow he'd get everything shipshape and back on course.

Tomorrow. Or next week for certain.

IT HAD FELT good to be out walking, Cléo thought, as she reached the door of the house she'd shared with Philippe. And the owner of the pastry shop had been most sympathetic, offering his condolences on the prince's death and not even charging her for the petits fours she'd be bringing with her on her visit to Christine later that afternoon.

"But leave the cake box on the table here," she told Georges when he took her cloak, "as I'll be going out again in an hour."

"Yes, Madame." The manservant bowed, and she suppressed a sigh. He'd always rather despised her for not loving his master more totally, and she could hardly blame him. Still, at least *his* future was no problem. He'd easily find employment in some great house in Mayfair. Philippe had probably already written him a reference.

But why, after putting away her cloak, had he come back to the front parlor?

"Madame?"

Perhaps he wanted to give notice today.

"Yes, of course, Georges." She motioned for him to

sit beside her on a cane-backed settee. He hesitated for a moment; to her knowledge he'd never sat down in the presence of an employer before. She congratulated herself for having chosen a stiff, straight-backed piece of furniture. He couldn't have managed anything more comfortable.

He allowed himself a small grimace – one corner of his mouth only – before seating himself. The grimace indicated mild appreciation and not a little surprise, at her grasp of the niceties of the situation. He hadn't expected so much, she thought, from a girl who still occasionally forgot her table manners.

"All right, Georges. What did you want to tell me?"

"Two or three things, Madame, that Monsieur had said. He was going to write a note, but he hadn't quite found the words. He wanted me to listen, while he worked out his thoughts. But it tired him. He put off writing the note, and, in the end, he didn't get the opportunity to write it. Still, I've decided you should know what he was thinking about."

She peered warily at him.

"He was in some physical pain," Georges continued, "though he was quite skilled at hiding it. He was very weak. It worried him, to think of leaving you alone."

She nodded. "He was very good."

His eyes told her not to interrupt. "Which is why Monsieur was grateful that you'd found someone to take care of you."

"*I* found someone?"

"He seemed to think so, Madame."

"What else did he say, Georges?"

The valet hesitated for a moment.

"He said he'd always believed you were searching for someone you lost years ago. And that the man in question must be of the same type. Very English, Monsieur le Prince supposed he'd be, with that eager, naïve English look about him."

"Monsieur le Prince was always a bit too subtle for me, Georges. After all, I'm English, too."

"He understood that, Madame. He accepted that. He wanted to tell you that he took comfort from the fact that he wouldn't be leaving you alone."

"Do you think he really was comforted, Georges?"

"I think he tried very hard to be, Madame."

"Thank you for telling me this, Georges."

"*Je vous en prie, Madame.*"

So Philippe had known. Not everything, of course, but as much as could reasonably be deduced.

Odd that he'd been able to read her so accurately. Before she'd met him, the other girls in the house had considered her a sort of actress – a performer, able to turn herself, chameleonlike, into whatever a particular man might want on a particular day. It was where her exotic nickname came from. Cleopatra, the slutty Egyptian queen who gave her men a lot of variety. They'd called her Cleo, before Philippe had Frenchified it to Cléo.

She'd always enjoyed her little acting turns, particularly in the red room, where you could draw upon the lessons life had taught you, to turn loss into lust or pain into power, but where it was you, at least for the duration of the performance, who kept all the power for yourself. She'd been glad Jack had asked for a taste of it. Not only would she give him a splendid time, but she'd leave him wanting more. And in truth, it had begun exceedingly well; she'd quite thrown herself into her role. Until she'd mouthed that bit about selling him to some lady, and she hadn't been able to continue.

Because in Jack's case there *was* a lady – a rich young lady, no doubt, with a father who'd buy her anything she asked for.

Anything or anyone.

She could still feel the moment when her little theater piece had turned itself upside down. She'd become choked by bitterness and envy, hating Jack's *young lady* with a cold, paralyzing, and all too real passion that took her breath away.

Quite spoiled his fun for him, she had. Spoiled *her*

fun too, for she'd been planning to teach him something quite new – force him to learn it, more like. But when the moment came – well, she'd be damned if she'd teach him to use his tongue to good advantage when the one who'd be benefiting from it would be the *young lady*.

Her mouth twisted. For in the end, which of the two of them was the one left wanting more?

So in the long run Philippe had been wrong. Yes, she'd once lost someone. But no, she didn't have anybody to take care of her.

Oh, she'd manage. Christine and Bernadette would help her. They'd plan it this afternoon over coffee and those petits fours. She'd walk to Christine's house, pass just a bit out of her way, and return the key she'd been carrying about in her reticule for... how many days was it now?

It was the decent thing to do. Leave the key in the entryway, where it had given her such a turn to see him that day.

The Housemaid's Room in the Garret

$\mathcal{W}$HEN HAD HE finally figured it out? There'd been no blinding flash of revelation, no single stunning moment when everything changed. Quite to the contrary, the knowledge had crept up on him, during his lonely days' wandering, from room to room and up and down the stairs.

And at night, too, in his dreams. He'd had some miserably troubled nightmares at first – pain, catastrophe, and of course the gargoyles. But as time wore on, his dream-self learned to ignore the obvious horrors, to search instead for a guide and helper. The little blue-eyed cat padded into view, peering at him from corners of dream rooms, stroking its flanks against a dream newel post. Sometimes it stood mewing, high up on the dream staircase, as though it wanted him to follow.

"All right," he'd told the cat one night. "All right, I'm coming." The next day he'd climbed to the top of the house.

To this tiny room. Rusty iron bed, straw mattress, one small high window, walls all mildew and crumbling plaster. Tin basin, cracked chamber pot. The memories had been faint – he'd had to keep calm and still, until they lost their timidity and agreed to take recognizable shape.

But now he could see them plain as day. He sat at the foot of the bed, eyes intent on a pair of figures: the boy at the door, nut-brown face and hair in a pigtail, the rest of him all grin and swagger and clearly the worse for drink; the girl with long black curls spilling across the pillows, covers pulled up to her neck. Her blue eyes were huge and dark; her skin almost translucent, lit from within by frightened desire.

Heartbreakingly young, caught motionless in time – did they exist, except in memory?

He didn't hear her footsteps on the stair until she was almost in view.

⟫⟫✳⟪⟪

"I CAME TO return the key," she said. "And then just to… to take a last look. I beg your pardon. I didn't know you'd be here."

He was silent for a moment. Then, "You have as much right to be here as I do. Come in if you'd like." He waved his hand at the bed. "Sit down."

"It's a very small bed," he added. "I didn't remember that. Well, of course, I didn't remember any of it, until –

I don't know – yesterday, perhaps…"

She sat next to him.

"But *you* remembered," he said. "You recognized me."

"The moment I laid eyes on you.

"I imagined you so often over the years," she continued. "Even when I didn't know if you were dead or alive, I imagined you, I couldn't help it. I'd see a man about your age and height, and with a certain look in his eye, and I'd think, well, it could be Jack, couldn't it? I'd look a bit closer; no, it wasn't you, it never was you. But I was always on the lookout, so to speak.

"Until last June when I saw the engravings in a print shop window, the portrait of you as the very model of a British naval hero" – Jack waved his arm, as though to dispel the vexatious image – "and the battle picture of you saving Lord Crowden, with the burning mast… and… and…

"Well anyway – her lip trembled – "I thought it could be you. Alive, by God. And when I saw you downstairs, I knew immediately."

"I thought you were offended," he said, "by how I was staring at you. Bloody indecent, the way I was staring."

"I was glad of *that* – though it would have been better still if you'd recognized me. Still, why should he, I asked myself. And what good would it do anyway?

Probably you forgot me as soon as you left here the next morning."

It hadn't, in fact, been easy to forget that night. Nights in his hammock, he'd think of anything at all – rather than try to reason it out, understand whatever it was he should have known how to give her.

But what good would it have done? The moment was lost, she was lost. Perhaps if he'd been brave enough to say something of the bewilderment he'd felt. But as he hadn't, the only thing to do was make himself forget her. For... for twenty-two years he'd kept her out of his mind and even out of his dreams.

"How bad was I that night?" he asked. "You can tell me; I'm prepared for the worst."

She laughed. "Not the worst. But pretty... *rudimentary*, I should say. Boyish, energetic, selfish – and also sweetly and terribly confused and ashamed of your own lack of... um, finesse. It was my fault, really. Some of the girls – and the madam too – warned me you weren't the best choice for my first time. But you were the one I wanted."

"*You* chose *me*?"

"The girls in the house would laugh at me," she told him, "the way I'd stare, if I was working anywhere nearby, when you came to the house with your mates. 'Ho, Jack,' I'd hear one of the other sailors calling to you, and I'd stop my scrubbing or hauling and just, just *stare* at you...

"They told me it was clearly time I had a man in my bed, and anyway, wouldn't I like to do some easier work than charring?

"I'd make more money, too, and have some nice things for myself. You're a pretty girl, Jenny, they told me. You could do well for yourself."

"*Jenny?*"

"Yes," she told him. "Jenny."

"Jenny." He tried it out and then he tried it out again. "Jenny."

She paused for a moment before continuing, smiling faintly, her eyes wide, as though she were seeing far into the distance. "'All right,' I told Mrs. Allen. 'Yes, all right I'll do it, but only if it's *him* the first time.' *She* laughed at me too. Well, she wasn't a bad sort, there's lots worse a girl could work for. And there wasn't much that went on that she didn't know – she said the girls told her you were even prettier with your clothes off, and that you could go on forever. 'He'll be anything but gentle,' she warned me, 'and not what anybody would call attentive to a woman's finer nature. No, he's not the right one, your first time, Jen,' she said. 'The girls've spoiled him – they let him pump into 'em as long and hard as he likes.'

"But I didn't care. And not, lord knows, because I was under any illusions about the profession I was entering, nothing like that. It was simply that... well, when I'd see you winking or grinning or larking about –

or clattering down the stairs to catch up with your mates heading back to the docks – just the *seeing* would create such a singular feeling in me, and that feeling was what I wanted. I became stubborn, wouldn't budge. With the result, finally, that instead of sending you to Beatrice's room that night, they sent you to me."

"I remember that part," he told her. "Mrs. Allen told me specially about the bargain I was getting; it wasn't every day that a customer got to have a girl totally fresh like that. She gave me more to drink, free of charge, and repeated how sweet and young and beautiful you were. She meant well, I think – I expect she was trying to educate me about a woman's finer nature. But she frightened me out of my wits. I'd never had a virgin, that's for sure. I wanted to refuse, but it was a challenge – a dare, like, and a confusion. I didn't know what to do. I was scared I'd break something."

"You were *supposed to*...well, to do something on that order," she said. "And you did. I don't know if you remember that."

"I remember taking off my clothes and getting ready to jump into bed with you. You were watching me, you looked a little scared but mostly calm... and... and happy... and *trusting*. God help us both, you trusted me, and I never felt so naked in my life... until last Friday, anyway, in the red room... You looked at me and you smiled and I pulled the cover off you and... did I say anything? I remember I wanted to say something…"

"You mumbled something. I chose to think that one of the words you used was 'pretty.'"

"Well, I was going to be gentle and sweet and kiss you…"

"You did kiss me. One time. Almost on the mouth."

"Before I climbed on top of you and forgot to be sweet or gentle. That's what I told myself afterwards, anyway, that it was all the drink in me made me forgetful, when the truth was – and I knew it when I saw you looking up at me –that I didn't know how to be equal to what you needed. Going to sea at twelve, like I did, a boy can learn to be a man among men, and be honored for it too. But to be a man with a woman? I don't mean the basic mechanics," he added hastily, "well, *that* was no problem, you know…"

She nodded.

"Right," he said, "Of course you know. And when I woke up the next morning," he continued, "You weren't there, and I didn't know if I was glad or sorry."

"I had to work. They hadn't hired a new housemaid to replace me yet. You were still sleeping when I went downstairs to light the oven, and by the time I had a moment to myself, you were gone. Which made me sad, but not entirely surprised. I'd heard your mates calling for you, after all. And then, of course, I was so awfully tired, having spent the night just looking at you while you slept."

"You deserved better."

"Yes, I know. Philippe taught me that, and over the years, I became brave enough – and even happy enough – to feel the… the…"

"The anger, Jenny?" It was painful say it. But remembering how she'd looked, the night she'd called on him at his lodgings – her back so straight, her eyes like the last embers in a heap of ashes – he knew that no other word would do.

She nodded slowly. "Yes, the anger," she said, "at life, you know. Even at myself sometimes."

If an inner hurt, he thought, could be as sharp as a boatswain's lash, it would be what he was feeling, hearing her speak of being angry at herself. Because he was all too familiar with that sort of anger.

And he also knew that if he allowed himself to lose her again, he'd never stop feeling that same anger.

Her hand had slipped into his. He grasped it for dear life.

"I didn't understand it at the time, of course," she said, "but now I can see that I wasn't only wondering if you were alive, I was wondering if you were… well, if you were really who I wanted you to be. Or if I'd simply taken all that fierce need to love and be loved and used it to create a happy, beautiful imaginary lover named Jack? Or was Jack really…?"

Sadly, he didn't know the answer to that question.

And so, all he could do was ask a question of his own.

"Would it be all right, Jenny," – he relaxed his hand a bit now, not to let go but to match the warm press of her fingers – "if I tried… if you gave me leave to try… if I spent the rest of my life trying… to be that man for you?"

Too late, he realized that he ought to have gone down on one knee, hopefully the good one. But her solemn, whispered "yes" was as good as if he had – for him, and for the shades of the two beautiful young people, no longer trapped in lost time, smiling their farewells as they faded from view.

≫≻≪≺

WITH A HOUSEFUL of large, beautiful rooms below them – not to speak of a large and well-sprung specimen of Elastic Bed – one might think it foolish that they chose to spend the rest of the day, and the night as well, on a thin and moldy straw mattress, in a horrid little room lit only by a guttering candle.

On the other hand, one might think it inevitable.

It was odd, however, Jack thought, how unusually talkative he found himself. Perhaps because he'd spent the week alone – that or the entirety of his life. In any event, he kept thinking of things to ask her. Silly things, he supposed, but…

"Did you mean it, back in the red room, when you said I was, you know, the rare sort of man…"

"…who likes to give a woman pleasure? Of course I meant it – well, you'd quite convinced me of it by then. Though" – how was it that he'd never noticed that shallow dimple in her cheek? – "I shouldn't object to a bit of additional convincing."

An extremely long kiss followed. A highly mobile kiss, his mouth beginning hot and eager on hers, then straying sideways to that dimple, before he made his way down her neck, breasts, belly, to end the journey, sometime later, quite convincingly elsewhere.

"Ha! Even surprised myself that time."

"You didn't surprise *me*, Jack."

BUT WHEN THE first stars showed through the small high window and she began gently disentangling his arms from around her, he surprised himself again by the urgency of his protest. "Wait, where are you going? You're not leaving, are you?"

"Not leaving" – she kissed him softly – "just going downstairs, luv. There are some cakes we can eat, and I'll get us some water to drink. Oh, and some lubricating ointment, if that's all right."

Only she didn't. She brought the rest of the butter, still fresh from the cool kitchen larder where she'd tucked it away last week. Giggling as she slipped back into bed, "I don't mind if we smell of it, do you?"

⫸⫷

AND EVEN AFTER the candle had burned itself out, as he basked in her touch, her belly sweetly curved against his side, he still seemed to need to speak of his astonishment. "I don't know how long I sat in this room before you came. Well, I could see the two of us so clearly, just as we'd been. You so innocent and me with hardly a scratch on me... Oh, no, Jenny, don't cry, I didn't want to make you cry."

"I'm all right...s-sorry...it's just, well, the years we lost... they're all gone..."

"They'd be gone anyway, even if we'd had them together. We'd still be lying side by side, preparing to sleep..."

"You want to *sleep*?"

"I'm afraid I'm going to have to. I've got my limits, you know."

Which wasn't really a bad thing, he thought contentedly. And she seemed to think so too, for when she spoke next, he could hear the beginnings of a smile shaping her voice. "I may be too excited to sleep. I'll probably stay up all night looking at you."

"You needn't. You'll be seeing quite enough of me. Tomorrow, and the next day and… well, as long as we two shall live, I expect. Every night, in this large, solid house. Of course, there *is* a problem facing us…"

"Only *one* problem?"

"Only one. To decide which bedroom shall be ours, and which, if there should be a family…"

"I like that problem. I shall give it some thought. You know, I wouldn't have been a good madam. I'd have worried so about the girls, their heartbreaks, and whether it would come out all right in the end…"

He kissed away a few more tears. "Go to sleep, Jenny dear."

⫸✦⫷

THEY STOPPED IN front of the mirror in the entrance hall the next morning to check their reflections. She straightened her bonnet, he his neck cloth.

"Not bad." He smiled – a private sort of smile this time; the grateful nation could take care of itself.

"Not bad at all," she agreed. "Quite attractive, for a couple entering their later years. Jack…"

"And Jenny. Common names," he said.

"Wonderfully common."

Common. One hears the word sometimes, rattling

through the language in phrases as various as common law, common sense, the Book of Common Prayer.

But as neither Jack nor Jenny was the sort of person given to pondering the mysteries of language, they merely smiled for the pleasure of a moment held in common. Before they walked arm in arm, out the door and down the steps of their house – say rather their *home* – into a busy street, in a no-longer-fashionable neighborhood, on a brisk and sunny London autumn morning.

Also by Pam Rosenthal

The Edge of Impropriety

The Slightest Provocation

Almost a Gentleman

Excerpt from *The Edge of Impropriety*

Winner of the 2009 RITA for Best Historical Romance

MARINA HAD TO smile at the picture Jasper made when she opened her front door to him. He was silent, but the pained little wince at the corner of his mouth spoke volumes as he stepped slowly into her front hallway. His muscles *were* stiff and sore, she thought, from helping the old lady yesterday.

How charming he'd been, how resolutely he'd put his shoulder against the clumsy old cart to move it. Softly, she put her arms about his neck to draw his head down for a kiss.

Usually they'd hurry each other up the staircase, but tonight, in the pool of moonlight coming through the high window, they kissed gently, tentatively.

"Oh lord," he whispered, "what must you think of me, so broken down and rickety? Perhaps I shouldn't have come."

"On the contrary," she replied, "I'm delighted. And especially that you arrived so promptly."

He groaned. "Took a cab. First time. Other nights

I've walked. Well, other nights I've *run*, actually, at least part of the way."

"Good for you, to indulge yourself in a cab for once. You can run again some other night and I shall enjoy imagining it. But if you can get yourself up the stairs tonight…"

"Or course I can." He thrust out his chin. "And you needn't think…"

"I don't. I shouldn't dare. But first, there's a bath for you. Come on. Here, take my hand. Let's get you into the water before it cools."

⟫⟫⟪⟪

JASPER HAD ALREADY seen the room where she bathed, the capacious, enameled tub standing upon tiles of green marble amid a little forest of waxy green plants and large potted ferns, and lit by a bank of candelabra set with thick, creamy tapers.

But seeing it – briefly, by way of a tour of her rooms – was one thing. Experiencing it as it was meant to be experienced – tub nearly overflowing with fragrant, soapy water, candlelight flickering through clouds of most air – was quite another. Having all this voluptuous luxury devoted to the matter of his comfort another thing still.

She was brisk and businesslike in the matter of undressing him – if you didn't count a stifled giggle when she came to the trouser button that had once been such an object of contention between them. After which – and after gently removing his spectacles and putting them safely aside – she led him to the tub and helped him lower himself into it.

"Is the temperature all right?" Her voice floated to him through the fragrant steam as she bustled about the room. "Because I've got a few buckets of cold water over there in the corner, and more water heating in front of the fireplace. I imagined you'd want it quite hot, though."

Yes. Very hot. He sank down more deeply into it, almost up to his nose.

"Lady Gorham," he murmured, "has anyone ever told you you're a ruddy angel sent from heaven?"

Laughing, a bit flushed, her face came into view amid the steamy air at the side of the tub. She'd taken off her dressing gown and pinned her hair into a careless knot at the top of her head, but curling tendrils were already loosening themselves about her neck and in front of her ears. The air smelled of the burning beeswax tapers; the water was scented with something he didn't recognize.

He sniffed curiously.

"Lotus," she said.

Closing his eyes for a moment, he sniffed more deeply. How singular that until this moment he'd never known what lotus actually smelled like. He smiled his astonishment, his pleasure. She was wearing a very plain, wholly untrimmed muslin shift. When she leaned over to kiss him, he could see her stiffened nipples, the flesh around them dark and distinct beneath the cloth's gauzy weave.

She ran her finger up his arm now, to his shoulder and around the back of it where it felt as though a great many muscles must attach together. He thought of men sculpted from bronze and marble, reaching back to throw a javelin, bending over to hurl a discus…

She pressed a fingertip – hard – against one particular spot and he stopped thinking of anything.

"Ouch."

"I thought that might be one of the sore places."

Her face, her breasts, disappeared back into the steam. He felt himself bereft. *Don't go, Marina*, he wanted to call out.

But he was glad he hadn't said anything when he felt her hands upon his back, her fingers suddenly slippery against the painful spots at the bottom of his shoulders. She must be using some sort of oil: it smelled of pine, like the resin the Greeks used to flavor their wine.

There was another smell, too. He took a long, astonished breath. "Wild thyme," he whispered. The stuff had been growing everywhere over the rocks, the day he'd found the Eros and Aphrodite in a remote Achaean village. There'd been a broken shrine; the statues had been buried for centuries beneath mounds of earth. Somehow, he'd known where he and the other men must dig. The moment of discovery had been thrilling, but for too many years since, he'd looked back upon it as theft, as one of his greatest shames.

And now he didn't have to. Because now – soon – he'd be making restitution. This morning he'd locked the Aphrodite away in the cabinet in his study and posted off his letter to Greece. The little kneeling goddess would wait at Charlotte Street until Dr. Mavrotis's arrival in London this summer. And after he met with Parliament and with Jasper and the other gentlemen of the Greek Emancipation Committee, Mavrotis would accompany the goddess back home.

Her fingers paused for a moment. "What did you say just now?"

"The scent. Wild thyme. In Greece. But please, don't…"

"No, after you said that. I thought I heard…" She chuckled. "No matter." She resumed her probing and kneading, of the knotted muscles and tendons.

It hurt a bit.

"Oh yes, that's it exactly, Marina."

It hurt quite wonderfully. As though the warm blood had once again begun coursing through his back and shoulders.

Perhaps it had – as indeed the blood seemed to be coursing more quickly to other parts of his body as well. He opened his eyes, glancing down past his belly to his knees rising out of the suds. And then finally, to another perturbation of the water's surface.

If *perturbation* it could be called.

"I think," she said, "it's time to give you a bit of a wash."

Excerpt from *The Slightest Provocation*

Nominee for the 2008 RITA for Best Historical Romance

"COME HERE," MARY said, "so I can look at you more closely."

In truth, to do more than simply to look: she'd have to employ all her senses to encompass the fact of Kit's presence. Her lips trembled, parting to take a deep heady breath of him. As once she'd taken greedy, icy gulps of water from the brook at the border of Rowen and Beechwood Knolls.

He'd taken hold of both her hands, holding them down at her sides, his own large, strong hands about her wrists. They exchanged a tiny, conspiratorial smile; she gazed serenely upwards, to take his measure.

The curtains stirred in a sweet salt breeze. A serene, temperate night; one wouldn't guess at the ferocious weather they'd been having just a few hours earlier. The fire burned low and even, its mellow warmth spreading upward around their legs.

Time was when the two of them would fall to sleep like puppies on the floor, in front of just such a low, comfortable fire. Sated by some newly discovered pleasure, exhausted and beguiled by some elaborately contrived private diversion, congratulating themselves on one or another highly athletic position they could almost believe they'd invented. Housemaids and butler would have gone to bed long before, or might even be beginning their workday, if Lord and Lady Christopher had made a really late night of it.

Shaking her hands free of his, she lifted her fingertips to trace the lines of his face: curl of lip, bump at the bridge of a nose broken so many years ago, swoop of eyelid fringed with straight, thick black lashes.

Difficult to cease her explorations, even more difficult to turn away. "I meant it," she said, "about my stays."

"I'm quite at your service," he replied, "but we'll have to start with your dress, won't we? Such a sweet pale green… it's very pretty on you."

She turned to allow him to get to the hooks at her back.

"Pistachio green, it's called." Uttered so softly that she doubted he'd heard her.

A ridiculous state of affairs in a civilized nation – how had it come to pass that a lady was unable to get out of her clothes without assistance? If assistance were what you'd call what he was offering.

Peggy would have had the buttons and hooks undone in a trice. But Kit wasn't bad at it. (*Of course he isn't bad at it*, she reminded herself. *It's not as though he hasn't unhooked a lady's dress during the past nine years.*) He fumbled now and then, cursing good-humoredly at the dress's formidable array of hooks, the buttons being more for show than function. Still, he had marvelously deft hands for a gentleman. When he'd been bored, he'd sometimes amused himself by carving little birds or animals out of wood.

She'd burned all the ones he'd left behind.

His breath – slow and warm on the back of her neck – came more quickly now, a low, cool whistle of triumph at getting through all those fastenings. She glanced sideways at the window, at their reflections against the black night sky. He was grinning, a slightly chipped right front tooth catching a ray of moonlight just an instant before he bent his lips to trace the curve of her nape. The tip of his tongue, rough as a cat's, began its nimble descent down the bumps at the top of her spine.

Her dress would have slipped down around her if she weren't holding it up, her hands on her breasts, the chambray falling in uneven folds – high around her shins in front, drooping down to the floor behind her.

He'd lowered her shift around the tops of her arms, his lips continuing downward, to her shoulder blades at the verge of her corset.

Her wings, he'd once said. If she'd had fairy wings, they'd have sprouted right there. Like water lilies, from those pads of bone and muscle.

You're a poet, she'd exclaimed, like Ovid. Don't tell my brothers, he'd responded—so quickly that they'd both laughed at how scandalized he'd sounded.

He must be surprised, she thought, at how primly she was holding the dress about herself. The two of them had been so careless back in Curzon Street. Returning home late at night, you could trace their path through the house by a trail of discarded garments – coat and waistcoat, cloak and lace mantilla... neckcloth and petticoat like snowdrifts on the entryway's black marble floor.

His hands had crept around her, to grasp hers, to pry them open and cause her to loose her hold on the fabric. *Oh, all right* – she sighed, and so, it seemed, did her gown, expelling a puff of air as it fell to the floor about her feet. Impatient and untidy as she'd ever been, she kicked the heap of cloth out of their way.

He'd cupped her breasts through the stiff fabric of her stays... no, wait, there'd been a sudden loosening – he'd taken a lucky tug at the drawstring. His inquisitive, leisurely fingertips moved closer to her skin, taking the time, she thought, to remember the shape of her nipples, which were stiffening at an alarming rate. He caressed her through her shift – she was wearing an old one. Damnable to be so short of clean undergarments, she thought. The silk had once been very fine but now it was almost threadbare – he could be touching her through a cobweb.

She must have leaned back against him. Her naked shoulders chafed against his coat; she could feel his hips, his belly – no use denying it, she could feel his cock – hard against her, through her petticoat.

"My stays," she repeated, in a more temperate voice than she'd have though she could manage. "Please, they're awfully tight about my waist. The… supper I ate, you know."

Forcing herself to take a step forward, she put an inch of space between their bodies, to stop him from continuing to press himself, in that disreputable, near-irresistible way, against her arse. Arms akimbo, she pushed her hands hard against the sides of her waist to relieve the tension of her flesh against the laces up her back.

"Ah," he murmured. His fingers had crept upwards from her breasts, to the shoulder straps, held fast with ribbon. No, not held fast, not now. She wiggled her shoulder blades, but he wouldn't be distracted from unknotting the strings at her waist.

"Ah yes, the supper you ate. I'd forgotten – no, in truth I've never forgotten – what a picture you make while you're enjoying your food. Press a bit harder for a moment, will you, so I can get a little slack on this loop… much better, thanks… do you know, Mary, that watching you eat, I found myself envying the capon?"

She smiled despite herself. "I expect there's rather a smutty witticism to be made from that."

"I should have thought you'd have made it by now."

"But you see," she told him, "what a staid, well-governed, and circumspect lady I've become."

Or at least a less vulnerable one.

He snorted with laughter and then took a breath. "Ah, got it, no more need of your help, thank you, Lady Chris…"

But she could already tell that he'd gotten it, by the sudden easing of pressure about her torso, not to speak of the impatient breaths he was drawing while he waited for her – to? Well, that was rather the problem, wasn't it? She'd hoped that this step of her hastily conceived strategy would have become clear to her when the need arose. Though in truth she remained unsure…

But she wasn't really obliged to do anything, was she? Even with the laces undone, she could keep her hands at her waistline and hold the garment's stiff canvas in front of her, as a sort of shield.

Hands firmly planted, she turned to face him. Her voice (she hoped) would issue light and abstracted, as if attentive to other concerns.

"Yes, well, my thanks for your assistance, Lord Christopher. Couldn't have managed without it, but as

I'm sure must be shockingly evident, I've had a most tiring day…"

His face darkened, jaw tensing, eyes slowly comprehending.

"…and so," she continued, "as I won't be needing you for anything else tonight…"

He snarled. "That was…"

You've got the advantage, she told herself. Have the courage to use it.

She dropped her hands and let the length of boned canvas tumble to her feet.

"…low!"

"No, they're not," she informed him (and rather coolly, too, she thought). "They – and I as well – have weathered the years quite admirably, thank you."

❯❯❯❯❮❮❮❮

SHE SUPPOSED (LATER, upon reflection) that she'd put out a hand then, as a gesture of conciliation or even apology. From which it reasonably followed that he'd taken it in his own, their fingers interlacing.

But as for how she had found herself so tightly and precipitously clasped against his front – in truth she wouldn't be able to render complete account of it. Though she was pretty sure it wasn't entirely his doing, now that his coat, waistcoat, shirt, and cravat were all pressed so importunately against her flesh, not to speak of his doeskin pantaloons with all their buttons below.

Disagreeable, him being so covered up: she should do something about it.

About Pam

A funny thing happened to San Francisco computer programmer and occasional essay writer Pam Rosenthal on or about the beginning of the twenty-first century: She became seized by an urge to write sexy period romance novels. She'd already published some erotica, buoyed by a wave of life-changing feminist discussion about what was possible, permissible, or just plain fun to say about female sexual desire. This led her to explore the history of sexual expression – and to think hard about what love has to do with sex and sex with love, and what sex and love have to do with freedom and respect between equals.

Or to put it another way, she'd begun taking on the big subjects at the heart of countless lives and also at the heart of romance fiction – at a historical moment when the romance genre was learning to write about sex in ways that spoke to women's whole selves as well as their fantasy lives.

Nurtured by this wide-ranging, supportive, energetic community of readers and writers, Pam wrote four romance novels and one novella. It was the experience of a lifetime, culminating in 2009, when *The Edge of*

Impropriety won Romance Writers of America's RITA Award for Best Historical Romance.

And then – sadly and surprisingly – she found that she'd said all that she had to say.

But the books remain. And Pam maintains an abiding respect for the writers who prevail over the long haul, a deep affection for those (like her) who have their say and move on, and a fascination with a genre that continues to grow and change, as it teaches itself to serve a wider, more representative community and a richer understanding of love, freedom, and respect for all of us.

Pam's a grandma now; retired from programming and novel-writing, these days she works alongside Michael, her retired bookseller husband, at their copyediting business, P&M Editorial Services. They love editing romance (check out their website at pmeditorial.com), and recently P&M have begun lovingly reissuing revised and expanded versions of Pam's romance fiction.

Visit Pam on the web at: pamrosenthal.com | twitter | facebook

Find out about P&M Editorial Services at pmeditorial.com

And (if you're of a mind) check out Pam's erotica-writing alter ego Molly Weatherfield, at: mollyweatherfield.com

"Thank you for giving me so much to think about. Thank you for challenging me and for moving me. Thank you for having the courage to break so many conventions, to write something so complex and unique…"

– *DearAuthor.com*,
about *The Slightest Provocation*

Afterword and Acknowledgments

When I got the rights back to this novella, first published in 2004, I thought that I (along with my copyediting partner Michael Rosenthal of P&M Editorial Services) would merely be fixing up those errors in grammar, syntax, or punctuation that might have slipped by the original copyeditor. And if I'd been in charge of this job, that's probably all we would have done.

But like my hero Jack, I found myself confronting a situation that was more than I'd bargained for, thanks to a partner who was wiser than I was. It was no big deal to take on the technical errors, from the smallest to the most cringeworthy (in the original, the walls of the entrance hall go from green to blue). But after we cleared away the obvious stuff, Michael's marginal comments grew sharper and more focused: from "What did he do with the cane?" to "Is this even physically possible?" to "Why did you choose this verb tense?" to "I don't think that's what he [or she] would have said here." Sometimes he was wrong (it *was* physically possible), but at best he made it impossible for me to ignore those places in the manuscript where I'd settled for a facile, unearned emotional interaction instead of going deeper.

Which was sobering, because when I first wrote *A House East of Regent Street*, I didn't think there *was* a deeper place to go, and this time around it hadn't even occurred to me to try for a revised, expanded version. The romance trope it's based on – an erotic quid pro quo becoming something more serious – seemed like a sturdy enough armature upon which to exercise my craft, but not a lot more. So I certainly didn't expect either Michael or myself to begin advocating for the characters, each in turn, and to demand that I play fair by them. Which only goes to show what a lovely, challenging, and complicated business it can be to write about love and sex, in close collaboration with one's all-time most astute reader. So yes – this is a revised, expanded version. Not a whole lot longer or a lot more sexually athletic (Jack and Jenny didn't need much help in that department). Just, I think, a little more coherent, a bit deeper. Thanks again, Michael.

And thanks as well to everybody who held my hand as I tiptoed into the daunting new world of self-publishing: Carolyn Jewel, Erica Monroe, Isobel Carr, and especially my gifted cover artist, Jessica T. Cohen.